Carlton Mellick III

"Easily the craziest, weirdest, strangest, funniest, most obscene writer in America."
—*GOTHIC MAGAZINE*

"Carlton Mellick III has the craziest book titles... and the kinkiest fans!"
—CHRISTOPHER MOORE, author of *The Stupidest Angel*

"If you haven't read Mellick you're not nearly perverse enough for the twenty first century."
—JACK KETCHUM, author of *The Girl Next Door*

"Carlton Mellick III is one of bizarro fiction's most talented practitioners, a virtuoso of the surreal, science fictional tale."
—CORY DOCTOROW, author of *Little Brother*

"Bizarre, twisted, and emotionally raw—Carlton Mellick's fiction is the literary equivalent of putting your brain in a blender."
—BRIAN KEENE, author of *The Rising*

"Carlton Mellick III exemplifies the intelligence and wit that lurks between its lurid covers. In a genre where crude titles are an art in themselves, Mellick is a true artist."
—*THE GUARDIAN*

"Just as Pop had Andy Warhol and Dada Tristan Tzara, the bizarro movement has its very own P. T. Barnum-type practitioner. He's the mutton-chopped author of such books as *Electric Jesus Corpse* and *The Menstruating Mall*, the illustrator, editor, and instructor of all things bizarro, and his name is Carlton Mellick III."
—*DETAILS MAGAZINE*

Also by **Carlton Mellick III**

Satan Burger
Electric Jesus Corpse
Sunset With a Beard (stories)
Razor Wire Pubic Hair
Teeth and Tongue Landscape
The Steel Breakfast Era
The Baby Jesus Butt Plug
Fishy-fleshed
The Menstruating Mall
Ocean of Lard (with Kevin L. Donihe)
Punk Land
Sex and Death in Television Town
Sea of the Patchwork Cats
The Haunted Vagina
Cancer-cute (Avant Punk Army Exclusive)
War Slut
Sausagey Santa
Ugly Heaven
Adolf in Wonderland
Ultra Fuckers
Cybernetrix
The Egg Man
Apeshit
The Faggiest Vampire
The Cannibals of Candyland
Warrior Wolf Women of the Wasteland
The Kobold Wizard's Dildo of Enlightenment +2
Zombies and Shit
Crab Town
The Morbidly Obese Ninja
Barbarian Beast Bitches of the Badlands
Fantastic Orgy (stories)
I Knocked Up Satan's Daughter
Armadillo Fists
The Handsome Squirm
Tumor Fruit
Kill Ball
Cuddly Holocaust
Hammer Wives (stories)
Village of the Mermaids
Quicksand House
Clusterfuck
Hungry Bug
The Tick People
Sweet Story

AS SHE STABBED ME GENTLY IN THE FACE

CARLTON MELLICK III

ERASERHEAD PRESS
PORTLAND, OREGON

ERASERHEAD PRESS
205 NE BRYANT
PORTLAND, OR 97211

WWW.ERASERHEADPRESS.COM

ISBN: 978-1-62105-174-9

AUTHOR'S NOTE

To be completely honest, I've never been a huge fan of the "portrait of a serial killer" genre. You know, stories where the serial killer is the lead character and you're supposed to somehow empathize with them as they hunt, capture, torture and kill their victims. It's not that I have a problem with cruel and sadistic characters, I just prefer stories that are told from the underdog's perspective, where all the odds are against them. Serial killer characters rarely have odds against them in these types of stories. The only time they aren't in the superior position is when they are evading the police. But even then they don't seem to be in that much danger because the cops in these stories are usually portrayed as clueless bumpkins who happened to stumble across the killer's path by accident and quickly find an axe in the back of their heads.

A lot of people love serial killer stories. Most of my friends love serial killer stories. But to me they're like watching a sports movie from the perspective of the undefeatable badass jocks as they utterly and flawlessly destroy the Bad News Bears. Who could be interested in a story like that? It would be too easy and boring. It goes against everything I believe good writing should be. And yet people still love these types of stories. It proves that there's no wrong way to tell a story as long as somebody out there finds it worthwhile.

As She Stabbed Me Gently in the Face is my attempt to write a "portrait of a serial killer" story that works for me without removing the elements that appeal to fans of the genre. I wasn't quite sure how I'd pull it off at first, because I wanted to keep the character true to the genre without pulling a *Dexter* (I do like the show, but a serial killer vigilante who only kills bad guys is too easy of an out if you ask me). By the end, the story actually did work for me. I hope it works for you as well. I might even want to return to this genre again sometime. Or perhaps try to tackle another genre that I don't particularly enjoy, like the "courtroom drama" genre. Actually, never mind. There's no way in hell I'll ever write a courtroom drama.

—Carlton Mellick III 12/29/2014 9:16 am

There is a fruit that only children can eat. It is the sweetest, juiciest, most delicious food that grows on the planet. Just one bite of its succulent pink flesh will put a child in a state of fluffy blissful joy that lasts for hours. It's called koka fruit, or koukyuu kahou, which means *forever happiness.*

Everyone remembers being a child and gorging themselves on kokas all summer long, making koka juice popsicles in ice cube trays and piling koka slices on top of mountainous ice cream sundaes. But then puberty sets in and the delicious flavor begins to fade. Through the teen years, kokas go from bland to bitter, bitter to rancid. By the time one enters their early twenties, koka fruit is no longer edible at all. It becomes poisonous. To eat just one bite would cause an adult to shiver and vomit for three days straight.

All that remains of the delicious flavor is the memory of having it as a child, and adults spend the rest of their days wishing more than anything that they could taste the fruit's sweetness once again.

CHAPTER ONE
TRAPS

Oksana Maslovskiy creates artwork that kills people. At least, that's what the newspapers say. Her art is literally deadly. Whether it's the poisons that she mixes into her acrylic paints or the plastic explosives she molds into self-portrait sculptures, she's always keeping the art world on its toes. It's why she has gained the nickname *The Duchess of Death*. It's why every gallery opening is always packed with reporters, collectors and curious onlookers. Nobody has ever been killed by any of her artwork. Not yet, anyway. But the idea of putting one's life on the line just to view her paintings and sculptures has excited audiences since she came on the scene five years ago.

"They really work? They can really kill?" Everyone keeps asking Oksana at her new opening. It's what everyone always asks her. But Oksana's response never changes. Without breaking a smile, without showing even a wrinkle of emotion on her face, she says, "Why don't you get close enough to see for yourself?"

Nobody knows whether she's joking or serious. Nobody has ever had the guts to test her claims.

All patrons must sign waivers before they're allowed inside the gallery. They're only permitted to enter at their own risk and they all know full well that stepping inside the doors will put their lives in serious danger if they're not careful. As long as they don't cross the red lines, their safety is guaranteed. But one step over and the gallery would not be held responsible for what happens to them.

"Human Mousetraps," says a woman in a loud red scarf,

reading the card next to one of the steel sculptures. "Is that what these are supposed to be? Mousetraps big enough for humans?"

The woman glances over at Oksana as though expecting the artist to answer, but she receives no response or acknowledgement from the lady of the hour.

"They don't look anything like mousetraps to me," said the woman.

Oksana steps through the crowded gallery like a dark queen striding down a blood-red carpet. The mob parts for her, instinctually getting out of her way as animals would flee a force of nature. She has that kind of power over people. She emits a kind of dark energy that prevents people from coming too close. That is, unless she wants them to. If she wants somebody to come to her all she has to do is look at them and they'll be reeled in more surely than a fish on a hook.

Edward Moore is about to learn exactly what it's like to be lured in by Oksana Maslovskiy. He sees her across the gallery, towering over the crowd. She's already six feet tall, but when wearing eight inch heels and with her hair in a platinum quiff that stands seven inches off her head, she looks like an ivory tower hovering over the sea of spectators. When Edward is caught in Oksana's gaze, he can't help but be pulled from one end of the room to the other. She doesn't stop bewitching him with her silvery eyes until he comes within two feet of her, then she looks away and pretends she doesn't even notice he is there.

"Ms. Maslovskiy?" Edward asks, his voice trembling. "It's an honor to meet you."

He holds out his hand, but she doesn't take it.

"I'm from Vide Magazine," he says. "Do you mind answering some questions about your new series?"

Oksana looks him up and down, then rolls her eyes. "If you must."

Although she acts disinterested, for Oksana this is as friendly as it gets. She's practically flirting with him. Although he's just an intern, Edward's magazine decided to send him to the opening rather than the more experienced staff reporters. They figured he'd have the best chance of getting something out of her, since everyone knows that Oksana has a thing for pretty young boys. She likes them naïve and timid, like little lost puppy dogs found on the side of the road.

"They're called human mousetraps, yet they don't look anything like mousetraps." Edward points at the closest sculpture. It's a black steel contraption as large as a tractor, shaped like an open human hand with cleaving blades for fingers. A piece of fruit lies in the center of it. "They look alien."

Oksana steps closer to examine her work, inching Edward backward. She hovers above him, looking over the top of his head at the sculpture, forcing the reporter to back up until he's dangerously close to crossing the red line.

"Perhaps they are alien," Oksana says. Her thick Ukrainian accent makes her sound almost like a vampire. She steps closer, putting her breasts at his eye level. "Imagine if a race of technically advanced beings as tall as skyscrapers conquered and colonized our world, and then reduced our species to mere pests living within their walls, stealing scraps of their food to survive. These could be the traps they'd set for the human rodents."

The look on Oksana's face frightens him. It's not what she's saying that scares him, but the way she looks at her sculpture and back at his body, as though she's imagining what it would be like if she accidentally shoved him over the red line into her steel trap. He sees it in her eyes. He sees her fantasizing about his flesh being crushed and torn to shreds within the massive claw-shaped blades.

"But what about the fruit?" Edward says, attempting to make a sideways escape. He points at the green and white striped piece of fruit in the center of the sculpture. "The bait for the trap is a koka fruit. Does that mean that these traps are designed for children? Only a child would go for a koka fruit."

As Edward tries to get around to the other side of Oksana, the crowd pushes him back. The only way out is a thin path between two large men, which Oksana quickly fills by stretching out her pterodactyl-wing arms.

"Not necessarily," Oksana says. "A parent might seek koka fruit to give to their child. Parents will do just about anything to make their children happy, even put their lives at risk to steal a koka from a killing machine."

Edward turns and looks at the sculpture.

"The blades look sharp." Edward leans in closer, his head slightly crossing the red line. "Why make them so sharp?"

Oksana steps forward and presses herself against him. Her small supermodel breasts poke against the back of his head—they're hard and pointy, like she's wearing a bullet bra.

"It has to be sharp enough to cut through bone," Oksana says.

As she puts a hand on his shoulder, Edward's instincts tell him he isn't safe. He can sense her desire to push him into the trap. People say Oksana always acts this way around reporters, like she wants to come across as sadistic and dangerous, but Edward doesn't believe it is just an act. She seems to genuinely want to see what would happen if he was torn apart by her murderous contraption.

Edward says, "That article in the Times last week said your machines can't actually 'kill people' as you claim. They're just for show. Do you think that will have any impact on your reputation?"

"Of course not." She leaves her hand on his shoulder for an uncomfortable length of time, as though she's completely forgotten about it. "Ever since I moved from modeling to art, the critics have been trying to discredit my work. That article isn't any different than the last fifty pieces they've published about me. Any intelligent person will write it off as desperate and mendacious."

Edward's awkwardness increases with every moment Oksana leans against him. With the ever-thickening gallery crowd raising the temperature of the room, he can feel sweat dripping down the artist's white dress shirt. He can't tell whether the body fluid is his or hers.

"But they had experts verify these sculptures couldn't possibly do as you claim," Edward says.

Oksana snickers against Edward's back. "Those *experts* only had access to photographs. I bet they also had made up their minds before they even looked at them."

A commotion erupts at the entrance of the gallery. Edward is just about to go completely over the red line when Oksana steps back to take a look at what's going on.

"What is it?" Edward uses the opportunity to get away from the sculpture, squeezing to the safer side of the artist.

"Something you'll want to see," Oksana says, keeping her eyes on the people charging into the gallery.

The security isn't able to stop them in time. Four punks push their way through the crowd, drunk and yelling belligerently. They're not uncommon types to be found at Oksana's shows, who usually crash her art openings for the free wine. But these four have something peculiar with them. Draped over their shoulders, they carry a naked mannequin with crude breasts and phallic imagery spray-painted on its chest and crotch, as well as the words *pretentious cunt* written on its stomach.

"Oksana Maslovskiy is a fake!" cries one of the punks—a skinny kid with purple dreadlocks, no older than twenty-two—as they charge toward the closest human mousetrap.

Edward watches Oksana's expression, surprised she's not in the least bit alarmed that the four punks are charging at one of her works of art, obviously intending to toss the mannequin into the trap to prove it doesn't work. And they couldn't have chosen a better trap to target, because of all the sculptures in the gallery it is the one that looks least likely to function. It's shaped like a massive spring wrapped around a chest of gears, appearing more like the insides of a music box than a mousetrap. A koka fruit is fastened securely on top of the device.

The crowd goes silent as the punks throw the mannequin

at Oksana's sculpture. When the figure hits, it makes a rusty clanging sound. Everyone's eyes lock on the sculpture, unable to blink, unable to breathe, waiting for the trap to spring. But nothing happens.

"See!" yells Purple Dreadlocks. "It doesn't work! She's a fraud!"

The gallery patrons drop their mouths and look at each other. A hipster giggles through his soul patch. An obese woman nearly spills her wine as she chuckles. Then the entire room bursts into laughter.

But Oksana doesn't laugh. Her expression hasn't changed one bit. She just watches her sculpture carefully, waiting with the patience of a black widow. Edward notices what she's looking at. Her eyes narrow in on the piece of fruit at the top of the sculpture. It has come loose from its bonds.

"They're all fake!" Purple Dreadlocks says, pointing and laughing. "Her art can't kill people. It can't even kill a fly."

Then Purple Dreadlocks runs across the red line and kicks the mannequin. The koka fruit becomes dislodged from the triggering mechanism and rolls to the floor. As the trap is sprung, it spins in a circular motion, releasing razor-sharp wires that slice through the mannequin like cheese. The punk leaps backward, barely dodging the wires that spiral through the air. When the machine returns to its original form, the mannequin falls into a pile of wood slices on the floor.

Nobody is laughing anymore. Their smiles have turned to shock and disbelief.

"They're real!" Purple Dreadlocks cries, his face filled with panic. "They really work!"

Then the punks turn tail and run out of the gallery, knocking over the stunned art enthusiasts on the way out.

But the punks aren't the only people escaping the gallery. Now that everyone knows that the sculptures are genuinely capable of killing, nobody wants to go near them. Those by the exit step calmly outside. Those who remain behind stay far away from the red lines around the sculpture.

"That's my cue to leave," Oksana tells Edward. "If you want to continue this interview, follow me."

Edward doesn't have time to respond before Oksana turns and walks away. Despite her towering height, she is able to casually sneak through the crowd without anyone noticing her leave.

Edward follows. He goes out the back door into the alleyway and meets Oksana at her car—a Swedish sports car as white as her hair.

"Get in," she says, stepping into the driver's seat.

"Where are we going?" he asks.

"My place."

As she shuts her door and starts the vehicle, Edward hesitates. He wants to go with her. Being invited back to Oksana Maslovskiy's place for a private interview is more than he, or his editor, could ever have hoped for. Still, he can't help but see her small bone-white car as yet another one of her murderous contraptions. He wonders if stepping into the passenger seat will trigger a steel blade trap that slices him into pieces as easily as that mannequin. Nobody would even see it happen through those black tinted windows. He would just disappear and never be heard from again.

Even though the windows are tinted, Edward can still sense Oksana staring into his eyes. Just as she did in the gallery, he is reeled in by her gaze. He finds himself opening the passenger door and crawling inside. Once seated, the door shuts and locks behind him all on its own.

That's it, Edward thinks. *I'm going to die.*

But no blades come out of the seat. No razor-sharp wires cut off his head. He's not dead. Not yet.

Oksana doesn't say anything to him for a while, focusing on driving away from the gallery and out of the art district without getting noticed. Edward tries to get comfortable as he sits in silence. The sports car seats are oddly shaped and seem to twist his spine and pelvis into awkward directions. For such a luxurious automobile, he would assume the seats would be extremely comfortable compared to those of economy cars, but these seem designed to torture passengers.

"Why did you run out of there so fast?" Edward asks, breaking the silence to get his mind off of the discomfort. "It seemed like things were just getting interesting."

Oksana stays quiet for another block, staring at herself in the rearview mirror while driving, fixing her dark eye makeup that doesn't seem to need any fixing.

"I was two seconds away from being swarmed by reporters," she says.

"And that's a bad thing? Most artists would kill for that kind of media attention."

"Oh, I'll get attention from the media," she says, then kisses her lips together in the mirror. "But my absence is the best possible comment I could give them after such an incident. It's better to leave them wanting."

"But you publicly proved that your sculptures aren't fakes. You made your critics look stupid. You didn't want to comment on that?"

"What would I say? Tell them *I told you so* and give them a wink." She removes a stray hair sticking out the top of her head. "That would be so tacky."

Edward nods. "I suppose so."

His discomfort in the seat grows into unbearable agony. It feels as though all of his weight is directly on his tailbone and he has to readjust himself every three seconds.

"Journalists have to be seduced and manipulated," says Oksana. "You can't just put out whenever they get horny for you. Nobody likes a media whore."

Edward realizes that the more discomfort he feels in his seat, the more Oksana watches him through the corners of her eyes. It's like she enjoys seeing him squirm. He wouldn't be surprised if she installed these seats for the sole purpose of tormenting her passengers.

"Is that why you only accept interviews with amateur reporters? Is it a tactic to make the big media jealous?"

"Maybe a little." She looks at him, ignores the road. "But it's mostly because I loathe interviews. The only way I can stand them is with a stiff drink and a pretty reporter."

"A pretty reporter?" Edward tries to hide his nervous laugh. "Is that me? Am I *pretty?*"

She puts her hand on his leg, not breaking eye contact. "You're absolutely beautiful."

Edward has never felt more awkward than he does now. His eyes caught in her gaze as her fingers crawl higher up his thigh. Without watching the road, Oksana could crash the car at any second, but instead of returning her eyes to the road her foot only presses harder on the gas pedal. They go faster. She doesn't break eye contact. It's like she's waiting to see how long she can keep Edward in this state of distress until he tells her to stop. But Edward can't tell her to stop. For some reason, he's unable to. As he looks her in the eyes, she seems so much more powerful than him. She's a woman, but she might as well be a four-hundred-pound football player. She might as well be Satan herself.

Just before slamming into a row of parked cars at a stoplight, Oksana removes her hand from Edward's lap and hits the brake, avoiding collision by centimeters.

"I'm just playing with you," she says. "You should loosen up."

While the car is stopped, Edward contemplates jumping out and running away. But that idea leaves his head almost instantly. This is the biggest opportunity he'll likely ever have. It could make his career. He has to see it to the end.

CHAPTER TWO
INTERVIEW

When they arrive at Oksana's place, Edward is surprised by the neighborhood she lives in. It's in the upscale market district near the university—a bustling area during the day when the shops are open, but completely dead at night apart from the occasional passing vehicle and the twinkling of a neon Budweiser sign coming from an empty bar at the end of the block. The surprising part isn't that she lives in such an upscale area, but that it's not really a residential neighborhood. Nobody lives there. Past sundown, the whole area is an urban ghost town.

"You live above a lingerie store?" Edward asks as she pulls up to a garage door between two clothing shops.

"I own the lingerie store," she says, driving down a ramp into a dimly lit basement garage. "And the shoe store next to it. And the jewelry store. I own all the whole building."

"I didn't know you were also a business owner."

"Then you didn't do your research. My name is on half the products sold on this block."

The basement grows darker the deeper down they drive until only her headlights brighten their path. Edward begins to wonder why her private garage is so far underground. He assumes there must be a public parking garage occupying the three levels above hers.

"To be honest, I haven't followed your fashion career very closely," Edward says. "In my opinion, I think your accomplishments in the art world are far more remarkable."

When they get to the bottom of the ramp, the garage widens into a space larger than a basketball court. There are more vehicles, mostly sports cars, parked on the far end of the lot. All of them belong to Oksana. It's like she has a different vehicle to match each outfit she owns.

Oksana nods at his comment as she pulls into a parking spot between a red Porsche and a black BMW. "That's why I like amateur journalists. They've yet to learn they're not supposed to have their own opinions." She turns off the car and looks him in the eyes. "Objectivity is such bullshit."

Oksana continues staring at Edward for an uncomfortable length of time. She looks as though she's about to grab him by the throat or kiss him, or perhaps both at the same time. Edward's peers at Vide Magazine already warned him this would happen. *You better watch yourself with her*, they said earlier that day. *A cute kid like you? She's going to eat you alive.* And his boss knew exactly what he was doing sending him to the gallery, kind of like sending in a sacrificial pawn to draw out the queen.

Edward breaks eye contact and exits the vehicle. But before he gets two feet away from the car, the headlights snap off and Edward finds himself in total darkness. He freezes mid-step, unable to move another inch.

"Whoa…" Edward says. "You really can't see anything at all down here, can you?"

His voice echoes in the darkness. Oksana doesn't respond, remaining inside the vehicle.

"Do you use a flashlight or something?" he asks.

Helpless without light, he has no choice but to wait for her. Three minutes pass and she still doesn't come. She doesn't answer when he calls out for her. He has no idea what could be keeping her.

"This is getting kind of creepy." He lets out a nervous snicker. "How do you find your way around down here?"

As he waits for a response, he feels Oksana's breath in his ear as she says, "I have a remote."

Then the basement garage brightens and Edward finds himself only inches away from the artist. He has no idea how she was able to exit the vehicle and sneak up on him without detection, especially in those heels. He wonders how long she'd actually been lurking in the dark next to him.

"How long have you been standing there?" he asks, looking over at the remote light switch attached to her keychain.

She doesn't respond, motioning with her chin in the direction of the elevator. "This way."

Their footsteps echo as they cross the lot. The garage seems even creepier than it did with the lights off. It isn't just a place for Oksana's automobiles. The garage is also a storage area for mannequins. Half the lot is filled with an army of white naked bodies posed in different positions. Despite their blank featureless facial expressions, they seem to stare at Edward as he passes them by.

"Do you feel safe living here?" Edward asks, as they arrive at the elevator on the far end of the lot.

"Sure. Why wouldn't I?"

"Nobody else lives on this side of town. It's deserted. Anything could happen to you and nobody would ever know."

"What could possibly happen to me?" She hits the UP button and waits for the elevator.

"Well, what if somebody followed you into the garage? They could trap you down here."

"Would I be trapped or would they? I'm the one who controls the lights down here. I'm the one who knows my way around."

"What if you were targeted by a stalker or a serial killer?" Edward asks. "They still haven't caught the Night Viper."

"The Night Viper?" She laughs at the idea. "Why would I be worried about him? He only kills men."

"So far," Edward says.

The elevator opens and they step inside. It's a freight elevator large enough to carry Oksana's sculptures, large enough to drive a car into.

"Trust me," she says. "I have nothing to worry about. You, on the other hand, *should* be worried. You're exactly the kind of victim the Night Viper targets."

Edward nods.

"I know. My mother calls me every day, begging me not to go out at night without a group of friends."

"You have a smart mother."

Oksana hits the switch on her remote, turning off the lights in the garage as the elevator doors close.

"What I want to know is why the press always says the Night Viper is a man," Edward says. "It could easily be a woman."

"But serial killers are always men."

"Not always. Women can be just as psychotic as men. My brother's girlfriend, for instance. That woman is bat shit crazy. Once she tried to convince him to let her sew his penis to the side of his leg."

Oksana smiles. "But, deep down, don't all women want to do that to their boyfriends? There's nothing psychotic about it, apart from asking him permission first."

Inside Oksana's apartment, Edward feels like he's in a museum or the lobby of an upscale hotel. Her place is filled with art. All of it her own creation, and all of it just as deadly as the human mousetrap sculptures from the gallery opening.

"Would you like a drink?" she asks him, standing behind a sculpture from her Venus Flytrap series—a similar concept to her human mousetraps but made with living plant life.

"Actually, I shouldn't be—" But before she hears Edward's response, Oksana disappears into the kitchen to make him a drink.

While he waits, Edward browses her art collection. He knows to keep his distance from each of them. There's no telling what they are capable of doing. Even the paintings and murals on her walls could be dangerous. He wouldn't be surprised if they shot acid into your eyes if you look at them too closely. Some of them might even be in her apartment because they're the ones deemed too dangerous to be displayed to the public.

"In here," Oksana says from another room.

Edward follows her voice into an area likely designed to entertain guests. Deep blue velvet couches look out of a balcony window, exhibiting a spectacular view of the city lights. The place hardly feels like an apartment. It's definitely not comfortable or homey. It feels more like a corporate lounge.

"It's a beautiful view," he says, looking out at the city.

"It is," Oksana says, but she's not talking about the view from the window. "Sit down."

Edward approaches his drink on the coffee table and picks it up to examine it. A green fruit cocktail with a piece of cactus stuck to the rim.

"Cactus kiwi," Oksana says, pointing at his drink. "It's my own special concoction."

He sits down and takes a small sip. The flavor is spicy, sour, sweet and bitter all at the same time. She stares at him, waiting for his approval.

"It's good," he says.

She nods. "It's strong, too."

Edward takes another sip. The piece of cactus resting on the side of the glass like a slice of lime scratches his cheek as he drinks. The needles have not been removed.

"Shall we begin?" Oksana asks.

She watches as he pulls out his notebook, her posture so stiff she looks like a porcelain doll on a shelf.

"Yeah," Edward says. A smile erupts on his face as though he just now realizes this is actually happening. He's finally interviewing the one and only Oksana Maslovskiy. "I have hundreds of questions I've been dying to ask you."

"Well, I'm not answering hundreds of questions," she says.

"In fact, the first question you ask that bores me, the interview's over."

Edward nods and flips through his notebook, seeking the best questions he's prepared.

"Okay, then," he says, taking another sip of his cocktail. "Why did you decide to move from modeling to art?"

Oksana tosses her drink across the table at him, splashing him in the face.

"That's it?" she cries. "Boring me to death with only the first question?"

Edward sits there in shock, dripping with cactus kiwi juice. His notes are soaked. His clothes wet.

Oksana sets the empty glass on the table, fully composed as though her outburst never happened.

"You can do better than that," she says. "I'll give you one more chance, but if I get a single question that I've been asked a dozen times before I'm kicking you out in the street."

Edward wipes the drink out of his eyes. "Okay…"

He closes his notebook and puts it down on the table. He realizes there's nothing in there worth asking anymore.

"Well?" Oksana says, her eyebrows raised high on her forehead.

As he hesitates, still thinking of what question to ask, she says, "I don't have all night."

"How about this one…"

He pauses to take a large sip of his cocktail. Then he asks, "How much did you pay those kids to crash your art opening?"

Oksana stares at him for a moment, then laughs. "You think I paid those idiots to vandalize one of my sculptures?"

"Why not?" Edward shrugs. "You were just accused of being a fake by the Times. The only way to prove them wrong would be to do a demonstration. What better way to prove that than to trigger one of them during the opening? Not only does it show you're legit, but it also makes you a sympathetic victim of vandalism at the same time. It was a masterfully crafted publicity stunt."

"I underestimated you." Oksana smiles and points at him with a long silver fingernail. "You're a clever one. How come I didn't realize how clever you are?"

"You didn't answer the question."

"Do you really think that's a question I can answer? If I actually did orchestrate the incident, the last thing I would do is admit it." She pulls a bone-white handkerchief out of her pocket and tosses it at Edward. "But you've proved you're capable of asking interesting questions. Keep going."

Edward unfolds the handkerchief and wipes the fruit juice from his face and arms. Then he sits up straight, trying to mimic Oksana's rigid posture.

He asks the next question. "When you first moved from modeling to sculpture, you had an assistant named Benjamin Scott. Whatever happened to him?"

Oksana's expression freezes on her face, completely thrown off by the question.

"How do you know about that?" she says. "Nobody knows about that."

"He was at your first six art openings and was seen in public with you a number of times. Then he just disappeared. Never told his friends or family where he was going. His landlord never knew what happened to him. All of his possessions were left behind. His neighbors said he just vanished one day and never came back."

She smiles at him.

"You're good. I never would have expected somebody like you would be so resourceful."

"So where did he go?" Edward asks.

"Who knows," she says. "He just stopped coming to my workshop one day. I assumed I intimidated him away."

"Were you lovers?"

"Not exactly," she says.

"What do you mean *not exactly?*"

"The whole ordeal was far too embarrassing to talk about. Ask me something else."

"Very well," Edward says. He takes another sip of his drink and then picks up his notebook and opens it to a dry page.

She smiles. "Ask me something fun. You're clever. I'm sure you can come up with something *fun*."

"Okay," he says. "How about this…"

He pauses for a moment, looks up at her with his pen pressed firmly against the damp pad of paper.

"When did you decide to become a serial killer?"

Oksana's face goes blank. Then she laughs out loud. "Where in the world did that question come from?"

Edward keeps a serious face.

"It seems that all this city's media ever talks about these days is the Night Viper serial killer and the renegade artist Oksana Maslovskiy," Edward says. "Won't it be interesting when they find out that these two people are one and the same?"

She points a silver fingernail at herself. "You actually think *I'm* the Night Viper?"

"I know you're the Night Viper."

She laughs at him again and leans back in her seat. "How absolutely droll. I had no idea you had such a dark sense of humor."

"I'm not joking," Edward says.

"This evening is becoming more interesting by the minute." She gives him a flirtatious smile. "But tell me, why do you think I'm the killer? The police are certain the killer is a homosexual male. There's no evidence pointing at me. Why would I risk my career to become a hobbyist murderer?"

"You're obviously fascinated by death," Edward says.

"*Everyone* is fascinated by death," she says. "If death wasn't fascinating, then my artwork wouldn't be as popular as it is. You'll have to do better than that."

"What about Benjamin Scott?" Edward asks. "He was your assistant and was the Night Viper's seventh known victim."

"Known? Benjamin disappeared. He wasn't a murder victim."

"His body was discovered, but it was so disfigured that he couldn't be identified. The police just know him as victim number seven."

"But you believe victim seven was my missing assistant?"

"Yes, I do," Edward says.

"How would you know?"

"Knowing that their son was missing, the police had Ben's parents come in to identify the body. They said it wasn't his, but only because the body was covered in tattoos. Ben's parents said he didn't have any tattoos. But he did, didn't he? He just never told anyone about them. *You* told him to keep them a secret."

"I told him?"

"It was *your* artwork tattooed on his body," Edward says. "Benjamin Scott wasn't just your assistant. He was your human canvas. You convinced him that because it was your art on his body, his skin belonged to you. He was not allowed to exhibit his body to anyone without your permission. Not even to his own girlfriend."

Oksana smiles. "I have no idea where you learned all this, but I'll admit it. It's true. I tattoo all of my assistants. Benjamin wasn't the first."

"So you admit you killed him?"

"Just because I tattooed Benjamin doesn't mean I killed him."

"But it does mean your assistant was the Night Viper's seventh victim."

"Perhaps," she says. "But just because I'm connected to a victim doesn't mean I did the killing."

"There's also the murder weapon," Edward says. "The police say the Night Viper uses a hand-crafted knife with an oddly-shaped blade. They say it's more like a work of art than a knife. They say only an expert at metalwork could craft such a weapon. You not only happen to be a master of metalwork, but you are an artist. If you were a killer it's just the kind of weapon Oksana Maslovskiy would use."

"I guess I would," Oksana says. "I have already crafted similar blades for my sculptures. It wouldn't be difficult to turn one into a murder weapon."

Edward nods his head. "Now you see why I came to the conclusions that I did. So, is my assumption correct? Are you the Night Viper?"

Oksana bites her bottom lip and leans toward him. "And what if I told you that I am? What would you do?"

"I would have a lot more questions to ask you."

"Really?" She puts both hands flat on the tabletop, like she's about to crawl across the table toward him. "You have a lot of guts for such a pretty young boy. If I actually was the Night Viper what makes you think you'd possibly get out of here alive? You're unarmed and all alone. In this neighborhood, at this time of night, nobody would even hear you scream."

"Who said I'm unarmed?" Edward pulls a small handgun from his pocket and places it on the couch next to him. "I'm not that stupid."

When Oksana sees the weapon, her smile grows wider. "So I see." She lets out a haughty laugh and sits back. "You better hope I am who you think I am or you're committing a very serious crime."

Edward doesn't even flinch. He's positive he has the right person. No matter what she says, he's not going to second guess himself.

"Very well," she says. "Let's pretend I am this Night Viper, this slayer of young men. Why put yourself in danger just to interview me? You're not even a real journalist yet. You're just an intern, aren't you?"

"This is the kind of journalist I want to be," Edward says. "I want to be a man who isn't afraid to put his life on the line for a good story."

"How romantic of you." She watches him carefully, examining

every inch of his body. "But you are afraid, aren't you? You can't even hold that pen without trembling. All your muscles are tense. Even with a gun, you look like a mouse in a cage."

"You're the Night Viper. Of course I'm afraid."

"The Night Viper…" Oksana rolls her eyes and looks out the window. "What a terrible name for a serial killer…"

"But they call you the Night Viper for a reason," Edward says. "The police say you attack your victims like a snake. You come at them from the shadows and stab them with a poison-laced blade. Your murder weapon is basically just a long metal fang."

Oksana casually pulls a blade from her waist. The sound of steel scraping against its casing echoes through the room as it is removed. Edward has no idea how she was able to hide such a large weapon on her person.

"It is, isn't it?" she says, gazing lustfully at the knife. "A poison metal fang."

It is the same weapon the Night Viper used to murder all those young men. And just as the police described, it is a work of art. The handle is a green tentacle that wraps around her wrist, becoming a part of her as she holds it. The blade is over a foot long, arched and angled very much like her sculptures. Getting stabbed by such a blade would rip apart your insides. It would mean a slow but certain death.

"Is that really…"

When he sees her holding the blade, Edward realizes it's true. She really is the killer. He wanted more than anything for his assumption to be correct, but there was always a slight bit of doubt in the back of his mind. Now that this has all become very real he doesn't know how to contain his anxiety.

"Yes, it's the same blade I used to gut all those poor innocent boys…" Oksana looks away from the blade and gazes into Edward with her powerful silver eyes. "So you wanted an interview with Oksana Maslovskiy the serial killer, did you?"

She stabs her knife into the table between them.

"Now you have one."

CHAPTER THREE
BIRTH OF A KILLER

Edward's hand trembles so severely he can hardly hold his gun. He hoped he wouldn't have to keep it pointed at her through the whole interview, but he's just not brave enough to leave it sitting on the couch next to him. Despite being in the superior position, he still feels as though he's at a disadvantage. Oksana is confident and relaxed. She doesn't seem too concerned about having a gun pointed at her. Edward, on the other hand, is terrified just by the look in her eyes. His heart beats so fast he can feel it in his chest. His vision blurs in the corners of his eyes. He's not sure how long he'll be able to hold out. But he wanted an interview with a serial killer. He's got to be strong if he plans to get through it alive.

"Why do you do it?" Edward finally asks. "Why do you kill?"

"Why do I have to have a reason? Do you think I'm one of those psychopaths who think they're doing God's work by killing random strangers? Or maybe because I'm an artist you think I do it as some form of self-expression? Trust me, it's nothing as romantic as that."

"But you have to have a reason," Edward says. "All serial killers have their reasons."

"Serial killers are so pretentious…"

"So you really don't have a reason?"

"I do it because I can," she says. "It's as simple as that."

"I don't believe you. You choose only attractive young men. There has to be a reason for that."

Oksana's smile drifts from her face. She pulls out a cigarette and lights it.

"It's sexual, isn't it?" Edward asks.

She takes a drag from the cigarette and slowly exhales.

Then she tells him, "It's definitely sexual." She ashes her cigarette into her empty glass. "There's nothing more intimate than killing another person."

"I've read that many serial killers are impotent. They aren't capable of having an orgasm through intercourse or even masturbation. Part of why they kill is due to sexual tension. It's the only way they can experience sexual release."

"The knife becomes the serial killer's penis." Oksana rests her palm on the handle of the knife. The wood splinters as she twists it into the table. "He stabs it into the woman's flesh as though he's fucking her. It's kind of pathetic, really. Is that what you think of me?" She lowers the handle of the knife toward her crotch as though it's her penis. "A pathetic sexually frustrated woman who wishes she had a cock?"

The gun shakes in Edward's hands as she grips the handle of the knife. "You tell me."

"I don't kill because it's the only way I can release sexual tension," Oksana says. "I kill because it's better than sex. Normal orgasms aren't good enough for me."

"So why do you tip your blade with poison? If it's so intimate I would think you'd want your victim's head to be clear."

"Their heads are clear enough," she says. "I use a poison that paralyzes my victims. It's not lethal. It attacks their nervous system, makes them incapable of escaping or fighting back. I'm able to take my time with them, sometimes spending hours taunting them, carving them up piece by piece."

"Like foreplay?"

"Exactly like foreplay. And though they can't move, they are completely aware of what's happening to them."

"Can they feel pain?"

"Oh, yes, they certainly can. Although they're unable to scream, I can still see the anguish in their eyes. It's incredibly satisfying."

"Are you sure that's not just fear you see in their eyes?" Edward says. "If they were numb to the pain they'd still express anguish just by witnessing their body being mutilated."

"I wouldn't know." Oksana shrugs. "You'll have to find out for yourself."

"What do you mean by that? Are you planning on stabbing me with your poison blade the second I let my guard down?"

"I would love to." Oksana smiles. "But I doubt you're brave or stupid enough to lower your little pistol for even a second. No, I don't plan to lunge at you with my knife any time soon."

Edward looks at his weapon. It's shaking in his hand so much he has to rest it on his knee.

"I don't need to," she says.

"What do you mean you don't need to?" Edward wipes sweat from his brow.

"I don't need to because you already have the poison coursing through your bloodstream."

A shiver crawls through Edward's skin as he looks at the half-empty cocktail on the table.

"Yes, I'm surprised you didn't notice sooner," Oksana says. "I poisoned your drink."

"You're bluffing," Edward says.

Edward's vision blurs again. His heart races. He thought this feeling was all just due to anxiety, but now he wonders if it was the poison. His breath weakens. His clothes go damp with sweat.

"I'm not falling for it," he says.

"Then wait and see if you don't believe." Oksana leans back and crosses her legs. "This batch was time-released. I didn't want you to go limp while the night was so young. It's not often that I get to enjoy my prey's company before I gut them."

Edward extends his weapon, aiming right at her heart as

his vision continues to blur. But he can't get himself to pull the trigger. He's not sure if it's because he's afraid to, unable to, or doesn't want to.

"What kind of poison is it?" Edward asks.

"Koka juice," Oksana says. "Completely legal, over the counter koka juice. Toxic to adults, as you know, but it's even stronger in its concentrated form. Koka extract is potent enough to paralyze."

"That's it?" Edward asks. He lifts his cocktail with his free hand and examines the glass. "It's just koka juice?"

"Enough to lay you out for hours." Oksana raises her eyebrows at him. "You're going to be so much fun to play with."

Edward raises his glass at her.

"Cheers," he says, then he drinks the rest of the green fluid.

He places the empty glass on the table and relaxes. His vision returns. His nerves unwind. He can't help but laugh when he sees the expression on Oksana's face.

"I'm sorry to disappoint you, Ms. Maslovskiy," Edward says. "But koka fruit doesn't have any effect on me."

She almost looks angry by the way she eyeballs him. Disgusted.

"How old are you?" she asks.

"Twenty-three," Edward says.

"Then why does koka juice have no effect? It should be poisonous to you at that age."

"I'm immune," Edward says. "I'm one of the rare few adults in the world who can eat koka fruit without any nasty effects. In fact, they're just as sweet to me as they were when I was a child."

"How is that possible?"

"For someone who relies on koka to get away with murder, I'm surprised you don't know more about the fruit. Kokas aren't actually poisonous to adults. It's an allergy to the fruit that doesn't set in until adulthood. It's kind of like poison ivy, which also isn't poisonous. The misunderstanding comes from the fact that the vast majority of people have the allergy. About ten percent of people aren't allergic to poison ivy, and a quarter of one percent of people aren't allergic to koka fruit. I'm part of the lucky quarter percent."

"Yes, you're very lucky." Oksana can't hide the look of disappointment on her face. "What a shame…"

"What about you? You're not lucky?"

"Far from it," Oksana says, pointing her cigarette at Edward. "I have terrible luck. In fact, I'm the opposite of you when it comes to koka fruit. They have been poisonous to me my whole life."

"Your whole life?"

"Even as a child, eating koka made me sick. Every time I tried it I became violently ill."

"That's kind of tragic. You really missed out."

"I missed out on a lot as a child. Not just koka fruit, I also didn't play with toys. I just didn't understand the fun of messing around with dolls and plush animals. Most of my childhood revolved around work."

"What kind of work?"

"I've been a professional model since I was six years old."

"That long ago? I knew you started young, but I didn't realize you started that young."

"My mother was the driving force of my career back then. She was Ukrainian and without a husband, and believed that my pretty face was going to make us rich. She said it was the *only* way a Ukrainian woman could be rich and I was naïve enough to believe her. So I spent my childhood working. It's as though I never had a childhood at all, forced to grow up as soon as I could walk on my own."

"So you never wanted to be a model?"

"Not in the slightest," she says, then takes another drag on her cigarette.

"You wanted to be an artist, right?"

"What I wanted was to have control," Oksana says. "I didn't want to be a walking coat hanger for some designer's new creation. I wanted to be the designer. I wanted to be a leader in the fashion industry."

"But you never pursued fashion design."

"I did, for a while, unsuccessfully. But then I learned the art world was much easier to manipulate. As long as you have the right presence, art is simple. You just have to convince people that you're a genius. If they think you're special, a one in a million, it's easy to trick them into believing your work is worth a lot of money. Talent is important, too, but talent will only take you so far."

"So you chose being the queen of the art world over a pawn in the fashion industry?"

"Something like that," Oksana says.

"Or was the real problem that you felt like a pawn to your mother?"

"Perhaps that's true." Oksana drops her cigarette butt onto the table without putting it out. A snake of smoke dances languidly between them. "I so hated my mother…"

Oksana stands up and goes to a wine rack in the corner of the room. Edward follows her with his gun.

"She had total control of me while she was alive," Oksana says as she stabs a corkscrew into a wine bottle. "What I ate, when I slept, how I sat, stood, or breathed, she dictated all of it for the first twenty-five years of my life. I was nothing but her pretty puppet. I had no life of my own."

Edward just lets her speak, holding his gun on her as she pours herself a glass of wine and throws it back like a shot of whiskey, then pours another glass.

"The only time I felt any sense of control was when I was with my little brother," she says. "He was so much smaller than me, so much simpler. Such a sweet little boy. And compliant. He did whatever I told him to do and he never complained. No matter how awful the task I forced him to perform, no matter how many times I hurt him, he was always obedient. I might have been my mother's puppet, but my little brother was *my* puppet. I loved him more than anything back then."

"You speak about him in the past tense."

"I killed him when he was nine," Oksana says. Her voice is

completely casual, without emotion.

"Why?"

"Because I wanted to see how it would feel to kill him." She takes another sip from her wine glass and returns to the couch. "I was stronger than him. I had the power to take away his life, but just knowing I had that power wasn't enough. I had to do it to prove to myself that I was strong."

"But I thought you said you loved your brother?"

"I did love him, but I loved killing him more." She drinks from her wine glass. "It was the first time I felt truly empowered."

"What did your mother do when she found out?"

"She was mostly annoyed that she had to cover up a murder for me. But what else could she do? I was her meal ticket. She didn't have a choice but to protect me."

"So your own brother was your first victim?"

"Yes, but he was just a warm up. When I was a teenager, I really started to blossom. Not just as a woman, but as a killer. I would lure boys back to my house when my mother was away, then butcher them on the kitchen floor."

"Did your mother know you were doing this?"

"Every single time. She was the one who cleaned up the bodies when I was through with them. I left them for her like presents, like a cat leaving a dead mouse on its owner's pillow. It drove her insane, but she wouldn't risk turning me in. I was already a successful model at that age and the more money I brought in, the more she needed me. It was the only bit of power I had over her."

"So you're just a victim of your upbringing?"

"I'm not a victim of anything. My mother was a selfish, overbearing woman and I wanted to be just like her. I was jealous of the power she had over me. I wanted to have that kind of power over people."

"But your mother wasn't a killer. She was just overly strict."

"Who said she wasn't a killer?"

"So you learned that from your mother as well?"

"Perhaps. I watched her murder my father when I was a

child. They loved each other once, when they were young. But my mother became mean and ugly with age, and love turned to resentment. He wasn't a faithful man. He was going to leave her. It happened the day he finally had enough of her bullshit and was on his way out the door, promising never to return. With all his belongings in two suitcases, holding one in each hand, he wasn't able to defend himself. She beat him to death with a hammer before he could get out the front door."

"And you witnessed this?"

"I was standing right next to him, hugging his leg, begging him not to leave." She changes her voice into that of a little girl's. "*Daddy, don't go. Please don't go.* Then my mother hit him in the back so hard I think she severed his spine. He fell to the ground with a look of shock on his face, unable to speak or scream as she hit him repeatedly in the chest. I remember the sound of his ribs cracking with every blow. I held his legs, crying for my mother to stop. *Please, Mommy, stop it. Please...* But she just ignored me. There was no emotion in her eyes at all, no hate or passion. She hammered his body as casually as she would a slab of beef with a meat tenderizer. When it was over, my mother looked at me as though she wanted to slap me for getting my new dress all covered in blood. Then she said, *help me clean this up.*"

When she finishes the story, she stares off into space for a moment and then brushes it off as though it was a mere anecdote.

"That's horrible..." Edward says. He shakes his head in disbelief. "I can't even imagine what that must have been like."

"Spare me your sympathy. I've done far worse things in my life than my mother did that day."

Then she finishes off another glass of wine.

"Such as?" Edward asks.

"Such as what?"

"You said you've done far worse things. What are they?"

"There've been so many. Where would I even begin?" She looks up in the air and scans her brain for a moment. "How about this: I once killed a boy after his college graduation ceremony."

"That's all? That's worse than a mother beating a little girl's father to death in front of her?"

"It is." Oksana nods. "If you saw the looks on his parents' faces that day, you'd realize it was much, much worse. I saw them after the ceremony, observing from a distance as I followed them across the college campus. You could tell by the wetness of their eyes just how proud they were of their son at that moment. They were obviously a low income family who never imagined they'd ever have a son with a college degree. The father probably worked three jobs to send him there. The boy probably studied day and night to get into such a prestigious school. You could just see what was inside their heads. They were imagining such a bright future for their boy. They saw him as a doctor, a lawyer, or even an astronaut. He would have the life they always dreamed of having. He was going to be someone special. Someone *great*.

"When he separated from his parents to use the men's room by the college bookstore, I went in behind him. I could hear his parents laughing and chatting outside the bathroom window, reminiscing about their all-grown-up-little-boy as I cut him open on the tile floor. He looked in their direction as he died, trying to cry out for help. But the koka juice paralyzed him. His parents were just on the other side of the wall but could do nothing to save him.

"As I left, I walked right past them and flashed them a big, satisfied smile. But they didn't even notice me. They were too busy wiping the tears of joy out of each other's eyes. I watched from a distance just so that I could see the looks on their faces when they finally realized what I'd done. It was one of the saddest things I'd ever seen."

Edward glares at her with disgust for a moment. He didn't have any words.

"How could you do that?" Edward asks. "How could you kill him when his parents were just outside the room?"

"Because it was more exciting that way. It was *naughty*. Like having sex with a strange man at a party while your boyfriend is waiting for you in the next room."

Edward doesn't know how to respond to that. "You're a monster."

"And you're fascinated by a monster." She leans back in her seat. "What does that say about you?"

"But why kill him at that moment? It seems deliberately cruel. If you have to kill somebody, why not kill somebody who deserves to die? A criminal. A rapist. A child-molester."

"As we've already established, it's sexual. I wouldn't kill anyone I wouldn't sleep with. I wouldn't sleep with some creepy child-molester. I like nice boys. The college graduate was cute and endearing to me. When I saw him with his parents, I fell in love. I just had to have him."

"Have you ever thought of giving it up? Going cold turkey?"

"I guess you can say that I did give it up for a while. A short while."

"Was that during the year the murders ended? The police thought you'd quit or moved to another city at the time. We finally thought the streets were safe."

"That was the time. It was for about ten months."

"Why'd you stop? Did you finally develop a conscience?"

"Not really. I didn't exactly quit by choice. I was kind of forced to."

Oksana's silver eyes narrow.

"How so? Were the police getting close?"

"Not at all. I met someone.""Who?"

"It's a long story. You might want to get comfortable."

"I'm comfortable enough," Edward taps his pen against his pad of paper. "Tell me."

"It was a dark and stormy night…"

"Seriously?"

"Just listen…"

CHAPTER FOUR
OKSANA'S STORY

I had an admirer who went to all of my art shows. We didn't speak before, not until that night. But I always noticed him watching me. He was cute. Not as cute as you. Not as young, either. He was in his mid-twenties, dark wet hair, snazzy round-lens glasses, and a black suit that fit him like a glove. He said he was French, but he looked more Asian than European. His facial structure was definitely Korean. He had these deep black eyes that made him seem far older than he looked. An old soul, you might say. I normally *hate* old souls, but he was different. He carried himself like a model. It was fun to imagine his small-framed body spread out across a concrete floor with my knife in his chest.

Our eyes met that night, when the crowd was getting thin. I waited for him to come to me. He was like a bashful little girl. Too shy to look me in the eyes, flirting at me with his long eyelashes. I've always liked men with long eyelashes. Maybe I'm a bit jealous because mine have always been so short. His nervous smile drove me wild.

I don't make it a habit of picking up men at my art openings. That's an easy way to get the police sniffing out my trail. But sometimes I just can't help myself. Exhibiting my art is a big turn on for me, and if I get worked up enough, I just need the satisfaction. I go for the prettiest boy in the room and catch him like a spider in my web. It's important nobody sees us together, just in case. I have to sneak him out the back when nobody is looking, get him into my car. Then I make sure his body is never seen again.

It was just like tonight, with you. I invited him back to my place for some late night cocktails. I drove him back here and he had the same nervous look on his face when he saw how empty this neighborhood is at night, how deep my basement garage goes underground, how trapped he was after the garage door closed behind us. The worried look on his face was absolutely delicious.

Unlike with you, I didn't bother taking him upstairs. I had to have him the second we left my car. He obviously was sexually attracted to me. He'd been lusting after me for months, so he didn't resist when I ripped open his shirt and kissed his neck. I laid him down on the concrete floor between two parked cars, pulled off his clothes and crawled on top of him. His erection probed my skirt as he tried to pull off my underwear, but I wasn't going to give him the satisfaction. I sat on his chest, held his arms down with my thighs. The hem of my wool skirt made his neck itch and I watched him squirm, trying to scratch himself using only his chin.

He was petite, almost half my size. I didn't have to poison him to prevent him from fighting back. I could just hold him down with my own weight. When I pulled out my knife, his expression was priceless. I stroked the cold metal against his cheek and watched him writhe beneath me, staring into those deep dark eyes of his. He knew at that moment what was about to happen to him and there was nothing he could do to stop it. I pressed the tip of the blade against his cheekbone and slowly pushed down on it. The metal pierced the skin, parting it effortlessly, digging its way to the bone. A stream of blood oozed down his chin. It was beautiful.

He wriggled and jerked under me, trying to kick me off. But then the poison hit him and his muscles went loose. I placed both of my palms on the end of the handle and lowered my weight on it, gently driving the blade deeper into his face.

It pierced his cheek and exited through the roof of his mouth. I pushed harder, forcing the blade into his tongue and lower jaw. Then I kissed him deeply, sucking on his lips, licking his split tongue, drinking his blood.

It was only foreplay. When I couldn't take it anymore, I pulled the knife out and thrust it through his glasses into his left eye. Not deep enough to kill him, but enough to split the eyeball in two. I could feel his quickening breath against my wrists as I twisted the blade in the socket, grinding that deep black eye into an unctuous lubricant.

I was getting wet. Not just because of how beautifully his flesh tore apart against my blade, but his rapid breathing pounded his chest against my inner thighs. His racing heartbeat pulsed beneath my skirt like a vibrator. I couldn't resist any longer. I drove my blade into his throat as I came, stabbing repeatedly into his face and neck until my crotch was drowning in a pool of his blood. When I finished, he was still alive. Just a little bit. Twitching. I wrapped myself around his small body and held him there, waiting for him to die. I closed my eyes, sighed against him, and listened to his blood ooze out of his throat, his heart slowing to a stop. Then he was quiet.

It's what would have happened to you had I acted sooner. When it was dark, down in the garage, you wouldn't have been able to grab your gun fast enough. That's what I was thinking when we were down there together. I couldn't decide whether to take you upstairs with me or tear you apart on the spot. And don't think for a second that I still won't. The night isn't over yet. One false move and you're mine.

I left his body in the garage. After such an orgasmic experience, I wasn't ready to clean up the mess. Nobody ever goes down there. Even if I left him to decompose, he wouldn't have ever been found. I came up here and got out of my blood-wet clothes. I took a warm bath. Then I spread out on the couch wearing only my robe, lit a cigarette, poured a glass of wine and closed my eyes, basking in the warm memory of the boy's death. It felt like I was wrapped up in the soul that I stole from him. All I could think about was his big dark eyes as he watched me kill him.

Then there was a knock at the door.

My eyes snapped open. It couldn't be. No one ever came to my door. It had to be my imagination. But there was another knock. Five taps. Somebody was definitely visiting me. But at such a late hour? The only way to that door was to take the elevator from the garage. Whoever it was, they had to know about the body.

The police? I thought. *Is it really the police coming for me after all this time? How could they possibly know? Was there a witness? Did some burglar sneak into my garage, trying to steal one of my cars when he saw me kill that boy? Did he call the cops or was he at my door with the intention of blackmailing me?*

I had no idea. There was no reason that seemed plausible.

I tightened the belt on my robe and went to the door. Five more knocks. When I looked through the peephole, I didn't see anyone out there. It was like a ghost.

"Hello?" I called out.

"Oksana Maslovskiy?" a voice said on the other side of the door.

His voice was soft. It didn't sound like a cop.

"Open the door," said the voice. "I want to talk to you."

"Who is it?" I asked.

"Don't be afraid. Just open the door."

I did as he asked. I opened the door. But what I saw was unreal. I was face to face with a ghost.

"Hi," he said, too shy to make eye contact with me for more than a second.

I couldn't believe it. Standing before me was the same boy

I just killed not twenty minutes ago.

"You…" I backed away. He had to be some kind of spirit come from beyond the grave to haunt me for what I'd done. He was no longer injured. The wounds on his face and neck were gone.

"Yes, it's me," he said.

His glasses were missing one lens from when I stabbed his eye and most of the buttons were absent from his shirt from when I tore it off of him. But the rest of his body was perfectly intact.

"Here." He handed me my knife, still covered in his blood. "You forgot this downstairs."

I didn't know what to say. It was the most shocked I've been since I was a little girl.

"I can explain," he said, and then invited himself in.

I just followed him around with the dumbest look on my face, still in disbelief.

He sat at this table, just where you're sitting now. He helped himself to a glass of wine and made himself at home.

"I forgive you for killing me," he said.

"Okay…" I said, sitting down across from him.

"It's not a problem at all. Because, as you can see, I can't be killed."

"You can't be killed?"

"That's right."

"You're immortal?"

"I guess that's what you'd call me."

"How is that possible?"

"It doesn't matter."

"Of course it matters. Are you some kind of vampire? Do vampires actually exist?"

I took a large sip of wine, trying to remember how much I'd had to drink.

"No, vampires don't exist."

"Then what are you?"

"I'm an angel. I've come here to save your soul."

I didn't know what else to do but laugh out loud after he said that. It was so ridiculous. I couldn't help myself.

"An angel? Are you kidding me?"

"I want to make a deal with you. If you accept my offer your soul will be saved."

"What if I don't accept?"

"Then I will leave and you will be beyond redemption."

I laughed at him again. "Are you serious?"

But he didn't have to respond to my question. His face was dead serious.

He said, "The deal is that you can kill me as many times as you want, over and over again, as long as you never kill another human being for the rest of your life."

I shook my head and poured a taller glass of wine. "You're insane."

He said, "I know you. I know who and what you are. I've been watching you. I don't think you deserve eternal damnation. You don't murder out of wrath. You murder out of love. To everyone else this is a horrible, disgusting thing. But I think it's kind of beautiful in a way. You're so full of passion. You just express your passion in a different way than others."

The way he spoke about it made me sick. If he continued I thought I was going to throw up.

"I don't want you to change," he said. "I just don't think innocent people should have to die to satisfy your needs. I'm here as a sacrifice for you. The perfect compromise. You can still kill to your heart's content. You can be as vicious and brutal as you want to be. You never have to worry about being caught by the police. And, best of all, you'll be redeemed in the afterlife."

I still couldn't believe it. "This can't be real."

"Trust me. It's very real. All you have to do is agree to the deal and I'll be your victim forever."

"I don't know," I said to him. "You are everything I want in a boy. I think I would love to kill you again. I'm still shaking from our moment downstairs."

He smiled. "Me, too."

"But I'm worried. As they say: If it sounds too good to be true, then it probably is."

"Just make the deal," the boy said, holding out his hand. "I promise you won't regret it. It'll be the best decision you've ever made."

"Are you sure you want this? I can get carried away sometimes..."

"It doesn't matter. I can't die."

"But you still feel pain, don't you?"

"I can endure the pain."

"Even if I cut out your eyes again? Or break your fingers one by one? What if I split your penis up the middle like a banana sundae?"

He looked down at his crotch for a second, hesitating for a moment. But then he nodded and said, "I'm willing to suffer all that you can give me. As long as I can save your soul. That's all that matters."

"Very well, then," I told him. "I agree."

The second I said the words, he leapt across the table and embraced me, crying into my shoulder.

"Praise God," he said, his tears wetting my shirt. "Your soul will surely be saved." Then he knelt down before me, like he was praying not to the heavens, but to his new goddess. "What a glorious day."

I hugged him back, imagining what it would be like to kill him again. And again. I still couldn't believe what had just transpired, but it was all marvelous at the time. I had my very own angel boy to do whatever I wanted with. He would never grow up. Never grow old. I could kill him as many times as I wanted to. The fun would never end.

"How am I supposed to believe any of this?" Edward asks Oksana as she takes off her shoes.

"Believe it or don't, but I promise it's all true."

"So you're saying one of your victims turned out to be an angel who couldn't be killed?"

"That's right." She removes her corset now. The white shirt beneath so wet with sweat that Edward could see her belly through the fabric and a dragon tattoo curled around her navel. "A real live angel from Heaven."

"What was his name?"

"Gabriel."

"So he wasn't just an angel, he was the Angel Gabriel?"

"No, he was a different angel named Gabriel. He said it's a pretty common name up there."

Edward just gives her a dumbfounded look. At first, he thought she was joking. But now he knows she's completely serious. She really believes she met an angel.

"I'm sure you think I'm insane," she says. "I thought I was crazy myself for a while. He had to be some kind of hallucination I was seeing. I thought maybe I had some deep, repressed guilt for what I was doing and conjured him from my imagination so that I could stop killing. But he was definitely real. If you met him you'd know he was real."

"I guess I have no choice but to take you at your word," Edward says. "It's not the story I was expecting to hear, but if it's the story you want to tell then I'll let you finish. I'll let my readers decide whether you're telling the truth, making it all up, or completely delusional."

"It makes for an interesting story either way," Oksana says.

"We'll see if my readers agree."

"What readers? When this is all over, what do you plan to do with my story? Write an article for your little magazine? Publish it in a book?"

"I'll have to see how it all pans out." Edward pulls out his phone and holds it up. "I've been recording everything you've been saying. When this is all over, I'll make sure your story is known in one way or another."

He sets the phone down on the couch next to him.

"So you still think you're getting out of here alive?" Oksana asks.

"I know I am," he says. "What I don't know is whether I'm going to turn you in or let you go by the end of the night. I guess it depends on how cooperative you are."

"As long as you have that peashooter pointed at me, I'll be as cooperative as you want me to be."

"You're letting me have control? I thought you hated being in a position of weakness."

"You actually think I'm in a position of weakness?" She chuckles at him. "That tiny weapon of yours has hardly any stopping power at all. If I wanted to, I could cut your throat at any minute. I might take a couple bullets, but you'd die a lot faster than I would."

"Then why don't you do it?"

"And have bullet scars for the rest of my life? I'd rather not. But I could do it, if you leave me with no other option."

"And how would you explain the bullet wounds in the hospital?"

"I was mugged, obviously. Or maybe a rapist threatened me with a gun and I just wouldn't give in. I can be very persuasive."

"Or maybe I'm a better shot than you realize," Edward says. "A headshot would put you down no matter how small the bullet."

"Sounds like we're at a standstill."

She puts her hands inside her shirt and removes her bra, pulls it out and drops it on the table. Edward can't help but notice her coffee-colored nipples through her wet white shirt. The nipples are almost too large for her small breasts, poking through the fabric, like they're pointing at Edward. He knows she's trying to distract him, make him uncomfortable in her presence. It's working. He blushes, shrinks in his seat. His gun seems so much smaller than it was a second ago. She has the upper hand once again.

"We might as well continue then," she says, rubbing her chest. She pretends to be wiping sweat from her clothes but is clearly trying to make her nipples more erect. "Where was I?"

CHAPTER FIVE
FIRST DATE

After I made the deal with Gabriel, I had to kill him again. Just to make sure it was all real.

"Right now?" he asked. The look of surprise on his face was priceless. "You just killed me an hour ago. There are parts of me that haven't fully recovered yet."

"You said I could kill you anytime I wanted," I told him. "And I want to kill you again. Right now."

I took the knife from the table.

Gabriel backed away. "But I thought we could talk more. Come to an arrangement. A schedule."

I shook my head. He was so nervous. Like a virgin who just paid for a prostitute and was too scared to even take his pants off in front of her.

"I don't do this by schedule. Take off your clothes."

He resisted at first, but I was able to get him out of his coat and shirt. I felt like a mother undressing my three-year-old. He flinched whenever I touched him. The memory of being stabbed to death downstairs was still fresh in his mind. But it was good that he was still afraid. I wouldn't have liked it if he was too compliant.

I laid plastic down on the floor and had him stand in the center of it. He didn't speak. Stiff as a board.

"You're so tense," I said as I came up behind him. "Relax."

I placed my hands on his bare shoulders and massaged him, told him it would be okay. I rubbed the tiny muscles in his arms and neck, gently digging my nails into his biceps. His skin shivered in my palms. I opened my robe and pressed my naked body into his, felt his chest expanding and shrinking against me.

"Loosen up," I said, picking up my knife from the floor. "Take deep breaths."

Gabriel closed his eyes and let his weight rest against me.

"Breathe in," I said.

He drew air deeply into his lungs.

"Now, breathe out," I told him.

He released the air.

I wrapped my arm around him, the palm of my hand on the top of his chest just below the collar bone, pulling him tighter against me. "One more time."

As he breathed in, I poked the tip of my blade into the center of his back. When he felt the cold metal against his naked skin, he recoiled, tried to jerk it away.

"Don't struggle," I said, gripping him tighter around the chest. "It's okay. Now breathe out."

He hesitated only for a moment. Then he did what I asked. As he relaxed his muscles and exhaled, I drove the knife into his back. His scream echoed through my apartment. I could feel it vibrating through the knife handle.

"Hush," I said, holding him firmly in place. "Don't scream. It's only halfway in."

He tried to bear the pain for my sake. His scream turned to a quiet whimper. I put my palm on his head, wiped the sweat from his brow.

"There, there, my angel," I said. "Calm down. You're doing so well."

He coughed up a glob of blood onto his chin.

I stroked his beautiful shiny hair.

"Don't worry. It'll be over soon."

For a few minutes, I just held him there on the end of my knife, enjoying the musical sound of his cries.

"Now one more time," I said. "Breathe in for me."

Gabriel coughed and convulsed, but couldn't inhale with my knife stuck in the back of his lung.

"You can do it, my angel. I know you can." I kissed the top of his head. "Just take one more deep breath."

His whimpers cracked and shivered as he took in as much air as he could.

"Now breathe out."

As he exhaled, I grabbed him by the hair and ripped his head back, then pushed the blade deeper into his chest. He fell to his knees and choked on the blood filling his lungs.

"Don't move," I ordered.

He tried to hold himself up as I lowered my weight on the handle, forcing the knife through his heart. I wrapped my arms around him and let him drop into my lap. Lying on the plastic-wrapped floor, covered in his blood, I rested my chin on his head as he died softly in my arms. It was so sweet. Like a dying newborn baby.

After he was done, I rolled him off me and stood over his naked corpse, waiting for him to come back to life. It was an unusual sight. For about ten minutes, he just looked like a normal dead body. I wondered if he was going to come back at all. The whole idea that he was immortal was absurd. Even though I'd already seen him come back once, a part of me doubted he was actually going to return to life again.

But it happened just as he said it would. The knife pushed its way out of his body by some invisible force. Then new flesh grew from the wound, sealing the hole. New blood pumped into his veins, the blood cells replicating almost instantly. His heart pulsed in his chest. His lungs expanded. When he woke up, he coughed chunks of meat onto the plastic.

As he gagged and spit, I knelt down behind him and stared at the wound. There wasn't even a scratch.

"So you really are immortal, aren't you?" With my index fingernail, I cut a thin red line across his back and watched as it resealed.

"That's what I said." He gasped with exhaustion. Regeneration seemed to take a lot out of him. "I'd never lie to you."

I pointed at the bloody plastic on the floor. "Put your clothes back on and clean this up. I've got a meeting in the morning."

Then I removed my bloody robe and left the room. When I returned wearing a nightgown that barely covered my crotch and legs, the gore-covered plastic was in a garbage bag by the front door and he sat on the couch, pulling on his shoes.

"So what's it like?" I asked him.

"What's *what* like?"

"Dying."

He looked up at me as he tied his shoes. "Like sleeping. Only more painful."

"What about Heaven? What's it like up there?"

He shrugged. "I don't know."

"What do you mean you don't know? You're supposed to be an angel. Aren't you *from* Heaven?"

"I've forgotten most of my celestial life since I came to Earth. In human form, I'm not capable of remembering God or Heaven. Human brains aren't sophisticated enough to process the true concept of Heaven."

"Are you sure you're an angel?"

"Well, of course. I remember some things. I remember—"

I interrupted him by dropping a pad of paper on the coffee table.

"I need you to write down all your personal information." I handed him a pen. "I need your home address, where you work and at what hours, the route you take home, your sleep schedule, your daily routine, and any other personal information that might be useful."

Gabriel just looked at the notebook. "What for?"

"So that I'll know where to find you when I'm hungry."

"But you don't need to find me," he said. "Just call me and I'll come over any time you want." He wrote his phone number down on the pad of paper.

I shook my head. "It doesn't work that way. It takes the fun out of the hunt. When I want you, I'll come for you. It'll be when you least expect it."

Gabriel looked at me with his puppy dog eyes. "But I thought we could arrange meetings. I could come over here on Tuesdays and Saturdays, or something like that."

"Is that how you want us to do it?"

"Yes."

"Well, I don't really care what you want. We do it my way or not at all. If you're going to have conditions then we might as well end this right now. I don't make compromises."

He lowered his eyes to the paper and wrote down his information. When I was satisfied he would do as I asked, I left the room to go to bed.

"Turn off the lights on your way out," I yelled back to him. "And take the garbage with you."

Then I shut the door to my room and went to sleep.

Gabriel worked as a waiter at a bistro downtown. The food was upscale but not quite a five-star restaurant. Not the kind of place I would ever step foot into. For the next few days, I watched him from a distance. I followed him home each night. I wore a hoodie and sneakers. You know, poor people clothes. And no makeup, so he wouldn't recognize me. But I didn't strike. He was expecting me and I didn't want him to expect me. I had to wait until he'd given up on the idea of being killed by me. I wanted him to believe I decided against our little arrangement. Otherwise, it wouldn't have been much of a hunt.

His studio apartment was modest and clean. He had very few possessions, but what he had he kept neat and orderly. He made his bed every day. His bathroom was so white that it looked like it belonged in a brand new hospital, despite being in an eighty year old building. There was only one of each dish in his kitchen, one pot, one pan, a knife, a spoon, and a fork. But he washed them every single night, even if he didn't use them that day. His hardwood floor shined with how often it was mopped.

I once watched him for a whole night from his apartment window. He didn't seem to have any hobbies outside of cleaning his house, brushing his teeth, and writing in a journal. Only his journal wasn't a bound book. It was a stack of paper, almost two feet high, on his desk. Each night, he took one piece of paper off of the stack and wrote down all of his thoughts from that day, plus anything out of the ordinary that happened to him. He scribbled on it, front and back, filling every inch of white. Then he dropped it into a cardboard box.

When he was out at work one day, I broke into his apartment to read his journal. I had to make sure he wasn't writing about me. Part of the arrangement was that he'd never tell anyone about me, or that we even knew each other. His writings had no mention of my name or the night he was murdered. But he did talk about a woman that he met that he described as *the most beautiful lady he's ever laid eyes on.* It was obviously me. Although there was nothing incriminating about the writings, I took all the pages pertaining to me anyway. Just in case. I burned them after I read them.

When I finally decided to kill him, everything was perfect. It was thundering rain outside, driving everyone indoors. I had the streets to myself. I stood on the sidewalk outside of Gabriel's place of work, letting the cold rain soak my clothes and skin, waiting for him to come outside. I couldn't resist anymore. Thunderstorms always got me in the mood to kill.

"Miss, are you all right?"

A young man with an umbrella who was walking down the sidewalk stopped to ask me this question.

I must have looked like one of those ghost women from Japanese horror movies, standing there like a statue with my wet hair covering my face. When I looked up at him, he smiled back at me. He was just my type. Thin. Pretty. Neat. The innocent look in his eyes excited me.

"You're all wet," he said. "Do you want to walk with me under my umbrella?"

I wondered if I should ditch Gabriel and go with this young man. He was so arousing to me. I imagined walking home with him under his umbrella, my arm wrapped around his waist, pretending to get closer so the rain wouldn't fall on me. Then I would put my knife under his coat and stab him in the midsection. As he writhed and whimpered, I would kiss him on the neck, grab his ass with my free hand. People walking by would think we were only lovers kissing in the rain. It was such a romantic idea. I so wanted to break the deal with Gabriel to be with him.

"I'm fine," I told the young man. "I'm waiting for someone."

"Do you want this while you wait?" he asked, closing his umbrella and holding it out for me.

He was such a sweetheart. You wouldn't believe how difficult he was to resist.

"No, thanks. I like the rain."

He nodded at me, then looked up at the sky. "Yeah, it's kind of nice, isn't it? After such a hot summer, it's quite refreshing."

Then he tucked the umbrella under his arms and walked away, enjoying the water pounding on his face. By the time he made it to the end of the block he was as wet as I was.

I immediately regretted not going with him once he was gone. He would have been such a perfect kill. But Gabriel was quite nice himself. When he was off of work, he went behind the restaurant and tossed three large garbage bags of old noodles and salad into the dumpster. He didn't see me coming up behind him. As he put the last bag into the dumpster, using both hands to reach the top of the pile of refuse, I wrapped my hand around his lips and cut into his armpit. His blood poured down his work uniform. He cried through my fingers as I stabbed deeper into the tender flesh below his arm. Then the poison took effect and he fell into me. I dragged him around the back of the dumpster and sat on top of him.

"Hello, my angel," I said to him, slowly cutting open his shirt. "I've been waiting for you."

Then I drove the blade into his belly. Though paralyzed, his legs still kicked and thrashed beneath me. I liked the feeling of his knees slapping against my wet ass. Due to his angelic immune system, the koka poison wasn't as effective on him as normal humans. The poison only weakened him. He still shivered and twitched as I twisted the blade inside of his body.

I didn't see the woman passing by on the sidewalk outside the restaurant. She paused at the end of the alleyway, staring at the movement coming from behind the dumpster. She only saw Gabriel's legs and my ass gyrating against the asphalt.

"What do you think you're doing?" the woman asked. She had the bitter voice of a daycare worker.

I stabbed the knife deeper into Gabriel and looked back at the woman. Then I laughed at her.

"Haven't you ever seen two people fucking before?" I asked her.

She dropped open her mouth with shock. Then I rubbed my crotch against Gabriel, pretending to be having sex with him as I twisted my knife inside his belly.

The woman was very strange. She didn't walk away as a normal human being would do. Instead, she stood at the end of the alleyway and scolded me for my rude behavior.

"You pigs!" the woman cried. "How dare you do that in public? What if there were children watching?"

I laughed at her and stabbed Gabriel again, sticking him with every thrust of my pelvis.

"Go fuck yourself," I told her.

She cringed at the F-word.

"I'm calling the cops," the woman cried, holding out her phone.

"Go ahead and call the cops."

Gabriel, with the knife sticking out of his chest, was far more worried about the woman than I was.

"Stop..." he said beneath me, grabbing weakly at my wrist. "You'll be caught..."

But it was too much fun to play it safe. The woman couldn't see the knife as I cut Gabriel, so I wasn't in any danger yet. She didn't dare come any closer than the edge of the alleyway. It was as though the act of sexual intercourse was so disturbing to her that she couldn't go within twenty feet of it. She even diverted her eyes when she scolded us.

The woman didn't call the cops, but held out her phone threateningly, pretending to press buttons as though that was going to get me to stop.

"Never in my life have I seen such appalling behavior," she yelled at me. "You call yourself a lady? You're disgusting. You're nothing but a gutter slut."

Ignoring the woman for a moment, I leaned forward and kissed Gabriel on the lips while driving the blade deep into his heart. He whimpered into my mouth as I kissed him, dying on the spot. I continued faux-fucking his brains out after he went limp.

"I mean it," the woman yelled. "If you don't stop, I'm calling the cops."

I put my knife away and curled Gabriel's body into a ball. Then I stuffed him in the corner, covering him with ripped open bags of garbage and old soggy piles of restaurant bread. Hopefully he would regenerate before anyone found him.

As I left the alley, I walked right up to the woman.

"You should be ashamed of yourself," she said to me. "I can't believe—"

Then she froze when she saw the state of my crotch.

"Is that…" she paused, shivering. "Is that blood?"

I looked down at the blood covering my lap and inner thighs. Then I smiled at her.

"Oh…" I said. "It got everywhere, didn't it?"

The woman looked in the alleyway, but couldn't see what had happened to the man I was with.

I said, "Maybe I shouldn't be having sex while on my period."

It was a ridiculous excuse, but the woman bought it. She stared down at all the blood in my crotch and put her hand over her mouth.

"Oh my God…" she cried, dry-heaving into her hand.

Then she ran to the nearest trashcan and threw up into the ashtray.

"You disgusting pig," she yelled at me, between pukes. "Piece of trash."

Then I rubbed my crotch with rainwater until it washed away, and walked casually down the sidewalk in the opposite direction.

"So the cops never came?" Edward asks Oksana.

She shakes her head. "The woman never even called them. She was just trying to threaten us into stopping. She had absolutely no idea what was really happening. Part of me hoped she would come into the alley to see for herself. Of course, then I would've had to kill her and I hate killing women."

"Why do you hate killing women?" Edward asks.

"I don't swing that way. Murder is like sex. I wouldn't sleep with a woman, so I wouldn't murder one either. Especially an ugly old bag like her. It would have disgusted me for weeks if even a drop of her blood touched my blade."

"Have you ever killed a woman before?"

"Thankfully not. I wouldn't hesitate, if I had to. Usually, I'm pretty cautious though, so witnesses are rarely a problem."

"So you got away with it? Nobody found Gabriel's body?"

"Actually, he was found soon afterward."

"By the woman?"

"No, a coworker. Gabriel was pissed at me for that. Actually, he was pissed at me for everything."

Halfway home, I heard footsteps trampling down the wet sidewalk toward me. When I turned around, I saw Gabriel. His clothes were ripped up. His body only half-healed, open wounds covered his torso and armpits. He would have been a frightening sight if anyone was outside to see him. He looked like a freshly turned zombie charging me, foaming at the mouth.

"Are you seriously following me?" I asked when he caught up.

I was not happy at all.

As he caught his breath, wheezing at the ground, not just because he ran all the way over to me but because he still had blood in his lungs, I scolded him further. "You're not allowed to approach me for any reason. I don't want us to be seen together in public."

I knew I was not recognizable in my current outfit, but I didn't care. I didn't want him to think we had any kind of relationship outside of being murderer and victim. I turned away from him and continued walking down the sidewalk.

"What the hell was that?" he gasped, following after me.

"What do you mean?"

I didn't look at him as he followed me. In order to continue the discussion, he had to walk behind me and talk to my back.

"That was insane. You could have been caught. You can't kill me in front of people like that."

"I thought it was fun. Didn't you think it was fun?"

"No, you could've gotten me fired. Patrick saw me out there in the garbage."

"Who's Patrick?"

"The sous chef. Do you know how embarrassing that was?"

I laughed when I imagined what that interaction must've been like.

"I couldn't even come up with an excuse," Gabriel said. "He just saw me passed out in the garbage and I had to pretend I didn't know what happened. Like I had a seizure or something."

"Why didn't you say you were mugged?"

"And have the cops come out? That's the last thing I would've wanted. That woman was a witness. If she was still around she might've claimed you were the attacker."

"Maybe. Maybe not."

"And look at my shirt," Gabriel said. "It's ruined. I need this for work. How am I supposed to explain this? It's going to come out of my paycheck."

"Not my problem."

"Look, you can kill me anytime you want, wherever you want, but my work is off limits."

When we arrived at an intersection, while waiting for the *walk* sign, I turned to him and said, "That's not part of the deal. If I can't kill you anytime, anywhere, without exceptions, then the deal's off. You should feel lucky. My normal victims don't get to whine about losing their jobs after I kill them. You know, because they're dead for good. They don't have the luxury of coming back to life like you do."

Gabriel's wounds finished healing in front of my eyes as he spoke to me. "I'm just asking you to be a little bit considerate. If I lose my job I could lose my apartment. Then I'd be some homeless man on the street. Do you really want a homeless man as your victim?"

I imagined him as a homeless man. Just the thought of it disgusted me.

"No, I absolutely will not dirty my knife with the blood of a vagrant. The deal's off if you start living on the streets."

The *walk* sign was blinking, but I didn't cross just yet.

"Then think before you attack me at my work."

"No, I will not make any compromises. It's your responsibility to make sure you're always employed. Get a second income as backup if you're worried about losing your current one. Make money online. Do whatever you have to. I don't care."

"Be reasonable..."

But I wouldn't listen to him. Just before the *walk* sign turned red, I crossed the street, leaving Gabriel behind. He didn't follow after me.

CHAPTER SIX
SECOND DATE

"Sounds like your relationship got off to a rocky start," Edward says to Oksana, holding out his phone to record every word.

She nods. "It did. After that incident, I really didn't think it was going to work out. I decided to test him. I wanted to see how far I could push him until he broke. If he had a problem with the way I wanted to do things then I wanted it to be him who got fed up and cancelled our deal."

"What did you do?"

Oksana smiles at Edward and rubs her knees.

"I fucked with his job. Since he didn't like that I almost got him fired the last time, I made sure every time I killed him that it put him at risk of getting fired. Not only was it to test his resolve, but it was also a way to teach him never to try to lay down ground rules with me ever again."

"It was his punishment?"

"He should've let it go. For the sake of variety, I never would have attacked him at his job again. If only he didn't complain his job wouldn't have been at risk."

Three days after the incident in the alley, I showed up at his restaurant in the middle of lunch. This time I wasn't in disguise. I came as myself, the one and only Oksana Maslovskiy. The staff was shocked that such a major celebrity would show up at their establishment. They put me at their best table, gave me their best wine on the house. The place was quickly packed with spectators and reporters. I'm sure you know, it's rare for me to be seen out in public like that. It was kind of a big deal. The manager took a picture of me and I think it's still up on their wall to this day.

Gabriel was the only one who wasn't excited to see me there. He was my waiter. The manager wanted to serve me himself, but I requested the cute waiter with the dark brown eyes. Just for that, the manager gave Gabriel quite the lecture. I could hear the old man in the back, yelling at the boy, telling him that if he fucked up that he'd be fired on the spot.

I almost laughed out loud when I saw Gabriel put on a large fake smile, pretending he wasn't completely pissed off as he waited on me.

"Would you like to hear the specialties of the day?" Gabriel asked me as he handed me the menu.

"No, thanks," I said.

Then he leaned in and whispered to me. "What the hell are you doing here?"

"Having lunch," I told him. "What does it look like?"

It was so cute watching him squirm like that. He was so nervous about what I was going to do.

"You can't be here," he said. "What happened to us not being seen in public together?"

"Whatever do you mean? We've never met before. I'm just having a casual lunch and you happen to be my server."

"But there're reporters here."

"Yes, your boss is shameless, isn't he? Calling them out in hopes that my visit will get him a little press... How absolutely desperate."

When Gabriel noticed his boss glaring at him, he changed back into waiter-mode.

"So what can I get you? A drink? An appetizer?"

I pushed the menu away. "I'm not hungry for anything in here."

"Then what would you like?"

I leaned in and whispered. "I would like you to meet me in the ladies' room in five minutes."

His mouth dropped open. "What? Now?"

I nodded my head.

"But I'm working…"

"I don't care."

"What about my boss? The reporters? Everyone is watching."

"There's nothing suspicious about going to the bathroom."

"But I can't go into the ladies' room. If I'm caught, I'll get fired."

"Then don't get caught."

Gabriel looked around the room at all the eyes staring at him. He was ready to collapse from the anxiety. It was so adorable.

"At least order something," he said. "The boss will be more focused on the cook than on me if I give them an order."

"Very well, tell the cook to surprise me. Give me his greatest specialty, whatever that is. I'm sure it will be dreadful, but it'll keep him busy for a while."

Gabriel left the table and went to the kitchen. His boss had a dozen questions and comments for him after that, so it took the boy a while before he made his way to the bathroom. He made sure nobody else was in there before he crept inside. With all eyes on me, he didn't have any trouble.

The manager tried to get an autograph from me, but I just pushed his pen away and said, "Excuse me."

Then I went to the bathroom. Gabriel was waiting for me in the stall on the end. I knocked twice on the stall door. He opened it, and I went inside, locking it behind me.

"This isn't a good idea…" he said, holding out his hands to stop me.

But I liked that he resisted. It only made me want to kill him more. I pushed him down to his knees.

"Don't get any blood on me," I told him.

"Don't do it if you don't want me to get blood on you."

"Just do what I say." I lifted the toilet seat. "Lean your head back."

He leaned back so that his head was over the toilet bowl. I draped my legs over his shoulder, straddling his head, and sat down on his chest. He gasped as the air went out of lungs.

"What are you doing?" he coughed.

"Shhhh…" I pulled out my blade and pressed it against his lips. "Be quiet. We can't let anyone hear us."

"I can't breathe…"

He was in a very awkward position, with all of my weight on his neck, crushing his spine against the rim of the toilet.

"Open your mouth," I told him.

He did as I said, obviously wanting to get it over with as soon as possible. Unfortunately for him, I was going to take my time.

I felt like a male celebrity. The kind who could walk into a restaurant, flirt with the cute waitress, and then secretly meet her in the bathroom for a quick blowjob. Only I was a female celebrity, and giving me a blowjob was a lot more bloody and quite excruciating.

I placed the blade of my knife inside of Gabriel's mouth, then used my pelvis to push against the handle. I jabbed it in and out of his throat, fucking him with the blade.

"Suck it," I told him.

He tried to wrap his lips around it, but the pain was unbearable, the poison was flooding his system, and the blade was just too damn big for his mouth. It sliced his lips in half.

Most of the blood leaked down his throat, but what escaped rolled into the toilet bowl.

"Careful," I told him. "Don't spit. You have to swallow. Swallow it all. If you get any on my skirt you'll regret it."

Then I pierced the roof his mouth, grinding my crotch against the curved end of the handle, forcing the blade slowly up into his skull until it pierced the brain. When he died, and I was finished with him, I propped his body up on the toilet and crawled out of the stall, leaving the door locked so that nobody would walk in on him.

As I washed my hands in the sink, another woman came out of a stall on the other end. I had no idea how long she'd been in the bathroom with Gabriel and I, but by the way she casually washed her hands next to me she obviously didn't know what had just happened. Perhaps she assumed I really was receiving oral sex from a rabid fan.

I went back to the table and waited for my food. After ten minutes of sipping wine by myself, the manager brought my lunch to me. It was Dungeness crab linguine with a Caprese salad. I wasn't very impressed.

"What happened to my waiter?" I asked the manager. "I asked for more water, but he just disappeared on me."

The manager was obviously shaken by the complaint.

"I'll get your water," he said. "Just a minute."

Then he rushed away. He didn't even give me an excuse for Gabriel's absence, obviously too furious to defend the boy.

On the way out of the restaurant, a reporter asked me what I thought of my dining experience. It was obviously going to be printed somewhere, so I decided to have some fun with it.

I said, "The food was exquisite, but the service was dreadful."

Both were lies, but I only wanted Gabriel to get chastised by the manager, not the cook. I was sure that would get him fired.

But, surprisingly, Gabriel was not fired for that. Business at the restaurant went up after my visit, so the owner didn't have much to complain about, and couldn't afford to lose any staff. Still, Gabriel was put on his boss's shit-list from that day on.

The next time I killed him, it wasn't at his job. It was on his way to work. I tried picking him up in my Porsche, but he refused to get in. He ran. I had to chase after him. I guess he didn't realize how fast I actually could go in that thing, because in less than a block I was able to run him over, crushing half his bones beneath the tires. I picked up his broken body, tossed it in the trunk and drove him out to the river.

On the bank, I finished him off using my knife, then tossed his corpse into the water. The current took him five miles downstream. By the time he recovered, he was six hours late for work.

I thought for sure he would have broken off our deal after that. I thought for sure he would've been fired. But he made up an excuse that got him more pity than reprimand. He said that he was hit by a car. The tire marks on his back were proof enough. He also showed up before he was completely healed, so his injuries were legit. Instead of getting fired, he got the rest of the week off. It was kind of annoying.

So I had to think of something much harsher than that. I had to think of what I could do to really test his dedication and his limits.

"You might want to call in sick for another week, because this could take a while."

We were at my place, in one of my workshops downstairs. I'd converted it into a kind of torture room, specifically for Gabriel.

When he saw the chains, saws, and meat hooks hanging from the ceiling, a worried look crossed his face.

"What's this all about?" he asked.

I was in a waterproof apron, pulling rubber gloves over my hands. "I want you to be my guinea pig. Your regenerative abilities intrigue me. I want to test their limits."

"What are you going to do to me?"

I sucked a lollipop into my mouth and spoke with the corners of my lips. "Everything I can possibly think of."

"It's going to hurt, isn't it?"

I pulled the lollipop out of my mouth, holding it like a surgeon's scalpel in my gloved fingers. "Oh, yeah. If I do succeed it will be the most painful experience of your human life."

"So what did you do to him?" Edward asks.

Oksana smiles and looks down at her hands, almost blushing. Edward can tell, whatever it was, she seems awfully proud of herself for thinking of it.

"I wanted to use his immortality against him," Oksana says. "His fast healing was too useful for him. It wasn't fair. I wanted to make him suffer for being unkillable."

"You got creative?" Edward asks.

"I am an artist, after all. Creativity is what I'm best at."

She picks up her knife and stabs at the air as she describes her process. "The first thing I did was cut him open, scoop out his insides and fill his empty torso with broken glass. Coming back to life was far more painful than being killed. His organs re-grew with the glass inside of him. His insides were sliced to pieces as they regenerated. For every part of him that was healed, three other parts were damaged in the process. His body needed to regenerate and regenerate again. Some shards of glass were forced out through his belly, others became fused with his organs. It was messy and painful for him. The agony dragged on for days."

"It sounds horrific," Edward says.

"Unfortunately, it wasn't very fun for me. It wasn't very arousing. I prefer cutting his flesh with my own blade. So that's what I did next. I started cutting parts off of him, starting with his tiny cock."

"You cut off his penis?"

"Yes, it grew back pretty quickly though. I had to cut it off every ten minutes. By the end of the night, I had a whole bucket full of dicks. The creative part of me wanted to sew them together, turn them into a grotesque sculpture, but I decided that kind of evidence would be best gotten rid of. So I burned all of the body parts I cut from him."

"How did he deal with it?"

"By the end of the week, I was sure I broke him. I was sure he was going to cancel our contract and refuse to ever see me again. I figured he would have left town and never returned."

"But that didn't happen?"

"No, it was quite the opposite. He told me that no matter what I did to him, no matter how painful or inconvenient, he was dedicated to being my victim. Whatever it took, he would save my soul. It was his sole purpose for living."

"So there was nothing you could do to scare him away?"

"Nothing. Nothing at all. At that moment, I realized that our deal could actually work out. He could be my eternal murder victim. It was almost like falling in love."

"You were in love with him?"

"Not in the traditional sense. What I loved was killing him. Nothing more than that. But I guess he was the closest thing to a long-term lover that I ever had."

"So it worked out for you? Your relationship?"

"For a while, everything was perfect…"

CHAPTER SEVEN
WRONG LOVERS

Gabriel was fun to kill. Before he entered my life, I only indulged myself maybe once or twice a month. But with Gabriel, I was able to do it every night. Sometimes several times a night. Sometimes I even killed him every other hour, waiting for him to regenerate and change his clothes so that I could eviscerate him once again. It was such a pleasure. He was my sweet little angel boy and he was all mine.

But he was a weird kid. Almost alien. I never knew what he was thinking. He didn't seem like what you'd expect an angel to be like, but he definitely didn't seem human. He never laughed, for one thing. He was always very serious. He was like a wild animal. You can tell when animals are worried or frightened, but can you tell when they're happy? When they're sad or excited? I'm not talking about dogs or even cats. I'm talking about mice, birds, rabbits. He was like that. When we were together, I felt like I was with a rabbit in human skin.

There was one other emotion that he expressed quite well. Loneliness. He was terribly lonely. I think being murdered by me was the closest he ever felt to another human being. It was the only time he felt alive. I enjoyed killing him, but I hated his attachment to me. He always wanted to spend more time with me after being murdered. The more needy he became, the more I realized that our relationship wasn't going to last.

He asked me to dinner on several occasions, while I was cutting him open in the park at midnight or while stabbing him to death in a deserted parking lot. Out of nowhere, he would ask me about my day, try to make small talk, when he should have been screaming in pain. It was very aggravating. It took the magic right out of murdering him. It made our time together feel mechanical, passionless. I had to remind him time and time again that I wanted nothing to do with him outside of murder.

But it wasn't his neediness that ruined it for me. I could handle his neediness. It was something else.

He often got erections as I killed him. I didn't think anything of it at first. There were many times where I took off my clothes and pressed myself against him before slicing him open. I sometimes even rubbed his dick with my ass before dropping the blade into his chest. It was natural for him to be aroused by that. But eventually, after five months of killing him, I realized that it wasn't my touch that aroused him. It wasn't my naked body pressed against his. It was my knife that turned him on.

One day I took him to a motel room and ordered him to take off his clothes and get on the bed. The second I pulled out my knife, his penis grew hard. I couldn't believe it. I was fully clothed, so I knew it wasn't my body that turned him on. He was excited to be stabbed.

When I pushed the blade into his stomach, he didn't scream in agony. He moaned with pleasure. I pulled it out and pushed it back in. His cries went wild with ecstasy. It was like he imagined my knife to be a penis. As I stabbed him, it was like I was fucking him with it. I couldn't believe I never noticed this before. I wondered if he always had a thing for being stabbed by me, or if it was a new thing. Perhaps he'd grown into a masochist to deal with the constant pain. Either way, it was a huge turn off for me. There's nothing appealing about killing a man who wants to be killed.

I pulled my knife out of his flesh and said, "Get out."

Gabriel sat up with a confused expression. "What do you mean? You haven't even killed me yet."

I cleaned the blood from my blade.

"I'm not in the mood anymore."

"Come on." He grabbed at my wrist, pulling the knife toward him. "Finish me off."

It was like I'd given him blue balls. He couldn't handle that I didn't see it all the way through to orgasm. When I looked him in the eyes, all I saw was desperation. He had a deep need for me to go all the way and not leave him hanging. I found it absolutely disgusting.

"Get away from me," I said, pushing him from my knife.

He sat on the plastic-wrapped hotel bed, staring at me. The holes in his chest already healing. "Don't you want to kill me?"

"Not anymore." I put the knife away, then grabbed my purse and coat. "Not at all."

And I left him there with that stupid, confused look on his face.

The next night, I watched him through his apartment window. He was playing a video of me on his television. A video of me killing him. I had no idea where the film had come from, but the fact that it existed at all made me want to drop him out of an airplane. From the perspective, it seemed as though he must've attached a miniature camera to his clothes. A spy camera. So Gabriel could re-experience being killed by me over and over again.

As he watched the recording, he slid his hand into his pants and touched himself. He played it in slow motion as the film version of me stabbed into his chest. Then he pulled down his pants and underwear, and masturbated furiously to the video.

It was disgusting. I was completely appalled. As he came, he moaned so loudly that it could be heard through his window, out in the streets. He kept his eyes glued to the screen as he died in the video. Then he started the film over at the beginning and watched it again.

When he went to work the next day, I broke into his apartment to steal the recording. But he didn't own just one. He had dozens of them. For months, he'd been recording being killed by me. It was revolting. I gathered up all of the videos I could find and took them, hoping that he didn't have any other copies backed up anywhere.

Back at my place, I watched each and every one of them. It was interesting seeing my murders from my victim's point of view. It was almost arousing to see what he was experiencing as I killed him. But the arousal faded whenever I thought of Gabriel getting off on being murdered. I couldn't stop seeing him masturbating to these images. I had no choice but to destroy all the videos.

"But I don't understand the problem," Edward asks Oksana.

She looks at him with a firm expression. "What do you mean?"

"The fact that he gets off on being killed by you should be a good thing. You're aroused by murder. He's aroused by being killed. You're perfect for each other."

Oksana's not very amused by Edward's comment. She lights a cigarette and blows a cloud of smoke into his face.

"I guess you could see it that way. Gabriel certainly saw it that way. But I'm not in the least bit attracted to a murder victim who enjoys being killed. I like sweet, innocent men. I like them pure. A man with a fetish for being cut and stabbed is a sexual deviant. A depraved pervert. I'm not attracted to such people."

"You sound like a hypocrite."

"Then I'm a hypocrite. I don't care. But the second I realized Gabriel enjoyed what I was doing to him was the moment that

I completely lost interest in killing him. He ruined an otherwise perfect arrangement."

I avoided him for weeks after that. Sometimes I saw him wandering the streets near my apartment or hanging around outside a gallery where my work was displayed, as though hoping that I'd want to kill him if I randomly ran into him. But killing him was the last thing I wanted to do, especially when I saw him putting so much effort into making himself available for the slaughter.

One day, I received a phone call from him.

"Aren't you going to kill me?" His voice reeked of desperation.

I was not happy that he called.

"How did you get my number?"

"I've been waiting for weeks."

"This is an unlisted number."

"I can come by later tonight… if that's okay with you."

"No, you cannot come over tonight. Or any other night."

"Why not? You haven't murdered me in so long. Surely, you're getting the urge to kill again."

"I'm not up for it."

"Are you okay? You sound depressed."

"I'm not depressed."

"Do you want to talk about it?"

Then I hung up on him.

He was right, though. I was feeling the urge to kill again. I just didn't want to kill *him*. I needed a new victim. Somebody fresh.

I went to the bar near my apartment, the one that was typically empty. But it wasn't always empty. On Thursday nights there was a beer special which attracted a lot of the local frat boys from the nearby university. It was not a typical hunting ground for me. I normally wouldn't search for victims so close to my place. But I was hungry and impulsive. I couldn't wait.

Wearing a long black wig and college girl clothes—tight jeans and tiny pink shirt that exposed my midriff—I entered the bar full of drunken college kids. My knife was in a backpack. Normally I custom design my clothes to hide the blade, but my disguise was too small to keep it on my person this time.

Most of the men weren't my type. Too athletic and aggressive. Frat guy types. Not somebody I could see myself getting intimate with. I prefer shy men, the kind who are vulnerable and awkward around beautiful women. I also target loners, and most of the college guys in the place seemed to know each other. There were also a few women and a couple of out of place old men.

It seemed like it was going to be a bust until I noticed a familiar face. Sitting by himself at the end of the bar was the young man I ran into outside of Gabriel's restaurant. The sweet boy who saw me waiting in the rain and offered me his umbrella. He sipped on a brandy as he sketched in a notebook with a well-chewed graphite pencil.

"I'll have what he's having," I told the bartender as I sat down next to the boy.

I made eye contact with him for only a second, but otherwise I didn't acknowledge him. I ordered the same drink as his so that he'd realize I'd entered his space and wouldn't be able to ignore me. It also helped me gauge his interest level in my company. If he wasn't attracted to me, or happened to be gay or in a serious relationship, I would know it without having to say a word to him.

"Here you go." The bartender set the brandy snifter in front of me and dropped the bill on the counter. As I lifted the snifter, examining the amber fluid as it rolled in the glass, I could see the boy looking over at me from the corner of my eye.

I didn't sip it or look back at him. I just waited for him to say something, gripping the glass tightly in my fingers. His eyes went back and forth between his sketches and my snifter. He had a question for me on his lips, but couldn't spit it out. That's when I knew he was definitely interested in me. He would be perfect prey.

I took a sip and savored the flavor. It was sweet and peppery. I hadn't tasted anything like it before. By the second sip, I could tell he was dying to ask me about what I thought of the drink but he still couldn't build up the nerve to ask me the question. He was acting much different than the first time I ran into him. In the rain, he seemed much bolder and socially adept. In the bar, he seemed awkward and meek. It was a major turn on. But I realized I would have to be the one to start the conversation.

"It's an interesting flavor," I said, still looking at the glass. "What is it?"

When I looked over at him, I could tell by the look on his face that he was surprised I was talking to him. He hesitated answering, as though he thought I might've been asking the bartender instead of him.

"I don't think I've tried anything like this," I told him. This time I stared him right in the eyes so he'd know it was him I was speaking with.

"It's fig brandy," he said, loosening the plaid scarf around his neck. "It's my favorite."

I nodded and rolled the liquid in the glass. "Fig… I hate fig." Then I took another sip. "But I like this."

He smiled and nodded and took another sip of his own drink.

"Where are you from?" he asked me, licking the spicy liquid from his lips. "I like your accent."

"I was born in Ukraine but I haven't lived there for a long time. What about your accent? Where are you from?"

"I don't have an accent."

"Of course you do."

"I'm from Seattle."

"Then it must be a Seattle accent."

"There's no such thing as a Seattle accent."

Then I laughed at him and shook my head. I was just messing with him, but it was a way to control the conversation. I didn't want him asking me questions. The less he knew about me the better.

I pointed at his sketchbook. "What are you drawing?"

He covered the image with his hand. "It's nothing. I just like to doodle."

"Can I see?" I asked him.

He hesitated giving it to me, so I pulled it out of his hands without permission.

"It's nothing, really," he said.

When I opened the sketchbook, I realized it was definitely not nothing. He obviously put a lot of work into his drawings. He also had a lot of talent.

"It's really sexy," I said to him.

"Sexy?"

The image was a surreal landscape. Mostly abstract shapes and textures, but in the form of a desert scene. Based on how he used shading and contrast, I could tell he was very experienced for his age. He must sketch these types of drawings all the time. Several per day. I was impressed and excited. There was nothing more satisfying than killing someone so special.

"Look." I pointed at the curves in his image. "The angles you use are erotic, sensual." I caressed my finger across his drawing, leaving graphite fingerprints on the page. "It's like the landscape is made of naked flesh. It's incredibly sexy."

He stared at his image with a smile, pleased by the discovery. He didn't realize what he'd been doing with his artwork until that moment. His technique was likely subconscious, completely by mistake. The boy must have had a lot of pent up sexual energy.

"Let me help you bring out the erotic features," I told him. I moved closer to him, pressing my bare hip against his elbow. Taking his graphite pencil, I drew on top of his image. I put more emphasis on the curves, added details to turn them into human muscles. I added breasts, penises, and pubic patches, but they were so subtle that nobody would ever have been able to recognize them on first glance. The sexual imagery would only work on a subliminal level, but it would still have a strong emotional impact on the viewer.

"That's amazing," he said with his soft eyebrows raised to the top of his baby-smooth forehead. "Are you an artist?"

As he held the image in his hand, I realized I would have to destroy the notebook after I killed him. My fingerprints were all over it. Or perhaps I would keep it as a souvenir. I wasn't sure yet.

"Yeah," I said to him. "I've done art professionally for a few years now."

"Professionally? You mean you make a living off of your art?"

"Yes, I guess you can say that."

He immediately introduced himself and shook my hand with his soft warm palm. His name was Ashley, or Ash. I preferred calling him Ashley. I introduced myself as Flora. He fluttered his eyelashes at me, smiling with his plump heart-shaped lips. I could tell his attraction to me increased tenfold knowing that I was a superior artist.

"I'd love to see your artwork sometime," he said.

"My art studio is just down the street if you'd like to..." As I said that, I looked out the window of the bar, pointing in the direction of my place, and saw Gabriel looking through the window at us.

"Yeah, I'd love to see your art," Ashley said. "Let me pay my bill and we can go."

But I wasn't paying attention to him at that moment. My eyes were locked on Gabriel's. The angel just stared at me, teeming with anger. I'd never seen Gabriel so angry before. It wasn't very cute at all.

"Don't worry about it. I'll get it."

I opened my wallet and threw down some bills on the counter. It was probably twice the amount owed for both mine and Ashley's drinks, but I wanted to get out of there as soon as possible and didn't want to wait for the bartender to give me change.

"Are you sure? I don't mind paying."

"Don't worry about it."

Before I could leave, Gabriel entered the bar and approached us. I tried to just ignore him.

He yelled, "What the hell are you doing?" as he stomped toward us.

He obviously wasn't going to be ignored. He knew exactly what I was trying to do with Ashley, and he wasn't going to let it happen even if it meant he started a scene.

"Let's go," I said to Ashley, pulling him by the wrist.

I wouldn't make eye contact with Gabriel and it obviously infuriated him.

"I'm talking to you," Gabriel said, grabbing me by the shoulder. "We had a deal."

I turned and looked him in the eyes. "I think you're confusing me with somebody else."

"You're not fooling anyone, Oksa—"

Then I pushed him. It was less a push and more an open-handed punch, shoving him into a rather large frat boy at the pool table. Everyone's eyes were on us by that time. Gabriel was seconds away from being jumped by twelve frat guys.

"Who's he?" Ashley asked.

I turned away and said, "No idea," as we walked out of the bar.

We only made it one block before Gabriel caught up with us. He was insistent on cock-blocking me. But this time he didn't go after me, he targeted the boy I was with.

"You seriously don't want to go back to her place," Gabriel said to Ashley. "She's not what you think she is."

Ashley looked at me, then back at Gabriel.

"This isn't even her real hair," Gabriel said, grabbing the wig off my head.

Ashley jumped back when he saw my long black hair fall to the ground, exposing a short platinum blond bob cut. He had no idea what was going on.

"She's a predator," Gabriel said to Ashley. "She only wants you for one thing, and it's not sex."

"What's going on?" Ashley asked me.

I shook my head at the artist boy. "Don't listen to him. He's crazy."

"*I'm* crazy? *I'm* the crazy one?" This was a side I'd never seen of Gabriel. He was not the person I thought he was at all. "You're the sadistic psychopath."

"Well, you're a pathetic masochist. You make me sick."

Ashley suddenly couldn't handle the situation he'd found himself in. He backed away as I argued with Gabriel.

Then he said, "I'm going to go."

"Yeah, get out of here," Gabriel told him.

I looked back at Ashley and held out my hand to him. "No, wait."

Ashley didn't stop backing up. "I just realized I've got some stuff to do. I need to get going anyway."

I don't know what happened to me next. Maybe it was sexual frustration, maybe it was misdirected anger, but I suddenly exploded at Ashley.

I yelled, "Get your ass back here, you little shit!"

And that was the end of my night with that sweet little

artist boy. He turned and walked away, as quickly as he could. I couldn't believe it. It was the first time anything like that had ever happened to me. I scared off my prey. I let him escape. And it was all Gabriel's fault.

"What the hell is wrong with you?" I yelled at Gabriel.

His anger calmed as Ashley escaped down the street. He looked at me with his old, angelic expression. "I did it for you. I was saving you from yourself."

"Saving me? What gives you the right to save me?"

"I'm committed to you. I want to make sure you get into Heaven."

"Do you know how much I needed that right now? He was so perfect. It would have been so beautiful."

He came closer. "It can still be beautiful... with me." Then he wrapped his hand around my hip and stroked my knife through my backpack.

As he felt the blade, he became erect. It was revolting.

"No, it can't." I jerked my backpack out of his touch.

"What's wrong? Don't you want to kill me anymore?"

"No, I don't."

A look of desperation filled his eyes. "But you used to love killing me."

"Killing you isn't fun anymore. You're not the person I thought you were. You're sick."

"But I'm perfect for you. I know I am. You have to see that."

I shook my head. "Just get away from me. I don't want to ever see you again."

I turned and walked away. He followed after me.

"But we have a deal," he said. "You promised you'd kill nobody else but me."

"Well, the deal's off."

"But don't you want to go to Heaven? You can still kill, you can still be what you are, with no punishment in the afterlife. As long as you only kill me."

I kept walking. There was nothing he had to say that would

convince me. "I don't care. I don't even want to go to Heaven."

"Why wouldn't you want to go to Heaven?"

"I don't believe in Heaven."

"But Heaven is real. I'm an angel. I know."

"Are you an angel? You don't seem like an angel to me."

"Of course I'm an angel. What else would I be?"

"How the hell should I know?"

Then I sped up, leaving him behind. He continued following me, watching me to make sure I didn't go in search of another victim that night, but didn't try to catch up. He waited outside of my apartment for three hours after that.

"He sounds like a nutcase," Edward says, as he organizes audio files on his cell phone.

Oksana shakes her head. "You wouldn't believe just how much of a nutcase he was. Over the next couple of weeks, he was even worse. He stalked me, followed me everywhere I went. Whenever I went after new prey, he would be there to break us up. He'd usually cause a scene, lie to my prey about how I had some kind of horrible STD or say that he was my husband and that we had a baby at home. Once he even told the truth and explained the violent things I had in store for my victim. Luckily, the guy didn't believe a word of it. He still got away, though. Gabriel was insistent on breaking up every possible murder attempt."

"Couldn't you do anything about it?"

"What could I do? Call the police? Get a restraining order against him? There wasn't much I could do. A few times, when I saw him following me, I'd pull him into an alley and stab him, just enough to fill his veins with koka juice. I figured I could lose him if I left him paralyzed in an alley. Then I could go after a new target without his interference. Unfortunately, tainting my blade with his blood was such a turn off. It killed the mood. I felt lost for those weeks. For the first time in a long time, I wasn't in control. I felt pathetic. Weak. I was a wreck."

"So what did you do?"

"Gabriel left me with no other choice. I had to try to get rid of him. For good."

After a dinner meeting with a gallery owner from Chicago, I came home to my apartment and found a note taped to the inside of my garage elevator. It was from Gabriel.

It read:

"I'm sorry things haven't been good between us lately. I know it's mostly been my fault. I haven't been the victim you need and deserve. I promise I'll be better prey if you only give me another chance. I care about you. I care about your soul. I just want you to be happy. Please, give me another chance. I'm sure you'll love killing me again if only you could open your mind and forgive me. It'll be just like it was before. You'll see. It will be beautiful again."

And then there was a postscript that read: "I left a surprise for you upstairs."

I was pissed. Did he think this note would change my mind? Did he really think things could just go back to how they used to be? He broke into my home. That right there was crossing a line that he really shouldn't have crossed. I didn't care if he was immortal. He was a dead man.

I ripped the note down and crumpled it into a ball. When I went up to my apartment, I noticed the door was unlocked. There was no sign of forced entry. He must have unlocked it himself. I'm not sure how he did it, but the little bastard had to have somehow stolen an extra key to my apartment and had it copied.

There was a trail of red rose petals on my floor, leading into my bedroom. I sighed so loud it echoed through the apartment, then I followed the trail to find Gabriel lying on my bed. He was naked with a gag in his mouth, his hands cuffed behind his back, his ankles cuffed to the frame of the bed, a big red bow around his neck. The mattress and floor were covered in plastic, ready to catch his blood without staining my bed sheets.

Another note was taped to his back. His eyes smiled at me as I read it: "You need release. Do with me what you will."

I tossed the note away. "Do with you what I will?"

I pushed him onto his side.

"Is that what you think I want in a victim? Offering yourself to me like a present?" I stepped around to the front of him. "I admit that could be a turn on for me." I pulled out my knife and pressed the cold metal to his skin. "That is, if you weren't an immortal…"

He didn't seem to be listening to me, more focused on my knife. It was obvious that he yearned to be cut. I put the blade under his chin and lifted his face to mine so that he would pay closer attention to what I was saying.

"You see, if a mortal offered himself to me, like a human sacrifice to his all-powerful goddess, *that* would appeal to me. A man who would willingly give his life to satisfy my hunger would make me feel incredibly powerful. It would be very satisfying. But what do you sacrifice by offering yourself? You can't die. You still feel pain, so that's a bit of a sacrifice, but now you enjoy the pain. If I were to kill you it wouldn't be for my pleasure. It would be for yours. And why should I do you any favors?"

He shook his head at me, trying to explain himself. But I couldn't understand him with the gag in his mouth.

"If you were mortal would you offer yourself to me? Would you let me kill you for real?"

Gabriel didn't hesitate. He nodded his head at me. I used my knife to pet his head like a good dog.

"Are you sure?"

He nodded again.

"Very well," I told him, stepping back. "I hope you're being honest, because that's exactly what is about to happen. I'm going to kill you for real this time."

He looked at me with a confused expression. He didn't quite get what I had planned.

"I'm not going to let you regenerate this time. After I kill you, I'm disposing of your body in such a way that it won't be able to come back."

The look of concern on Gabriel's face was delicious. He struggled, trying to break free of his bonds. It was the first time in a long time that I actually wanted to kill him.

"I don't know how I'm going to do it yet, but I've got time to figure it out. Whether I have to chop you up into a million pieces, burn you, dissolve you in acid, something has got to kill you permanently. And I plan to find it."

He whined through his gag and thrashed against the mattress. He kicked at the bed frame, trying to break the bars. But he wasn't getting free. All he could do was accept his fate.

CHAPTER EIGHT
BREAK UP

He wasn't moaning in ecstasy as I stabbed him. This time, he was shaking with fear. Tears rolled down his cheeks, his nostrils dripped with thin salty mucus. It would have been beautiful seeing him in this state, but I had the creeping suspicion that he wasn't crying for himself. He wasn't scared of dying for good. It was as though he was crying for me. Without using him as a permanent murder victim, he wouldn't be able to save my soul. I would be damned without him. I would kill other men. And the thought of me killing other men filled him with more anguish than anything I could ever do to him.

This thought took all the fun out of watching him squirm. After cutting into him three times, I was already bored. So I pulled back on his hair and slit his throat.

As he bled out, I said, "This is the last you'll ever see of this world. I hope it was worth it."

Once he was gone, I buried the knife deep in his heart. Then I tied it to his torso so that his regenerating muscles didn't push it back out. Using a handsaw, I cut off his feet first. Then I removed the cuffs on his ankles. I wrapped his body up in plastic, put him on a cart and took him down into the basement, into my makeshift torture room with the furnace.

Fire seemed like the most logical way to permanently kill him, so that was what I started with. I used the handsaw to cut him into small pieces, which wasn't easy at all. His body regenerated so fast that I had a hard time keeping up. By the time I cut off the third limb, the first would already have grown back. I hacked so many body parts from him that there wasn't enough room in the furnace to burn them all at once. I cut as fast as I could, but eventually my arms grew tired. My sawing slowed down. And when I was too sore to cut any more, all of his limbs had grown back. I was so frustrated I tossed the saw across the room. There was no way I'd be able to get rid of him like that. I had to think of another way.

As I waited for his limbs to burn so that I could dispose of the rest of his severed body parts, I noticed something I never expected. Something that caught me off guard. The other limbs, lying in a pile on the floor, were beginning to regenerate. I wasn't sure how they were able to re-grow after being cut away from his main body, but it was clear that an ankle was growing from a severed foot. Elbows were growing from a severed forearm. One arm was even growing what looked to be the beginnings of a torso.

Would they continue to grow if I left them there? Would a whole other body grow from the severed limbs? There were fourteen body parts on the floor. Would they eventually grow into fourteen more Gabriels if I didn't burn them in time? That thought sent me into a panic. One Gabriel was bad enough. I couldn't imagine what would happen if there were a whole army of them running around.

I shoved as many parts as I could fit into the furnace. Then I put a few more into a paint bucket, poured lighter fluid over it and set it on fire. There were still seven body parts left that I wrapped in an old coat and took upstairs.

I wasn't sure how to get rid of them. In my frenzied state, I tried everything, no matter how ridiculous. I shoved a leg in the oven and turned the temperature up all the way. I stuffed two hands into the toaster. I dropped fingers one at a time into the garbage disposal. Then I chopped up the rest of the body parts and flushed them down the toilet. Before I could get them all down, the toilet clogged. I was left with a slab of thigh meat. Not knowing what else to do with it, I tore into it with my teeth, chewed it up and swallowed it. I must've looked like a rabid cannibal as I sat on the bathroom floor, devouring the chunk of muscle as quickly as I could.

When I went downstairs, the fire in the furnace had gone out and the pieces of half-burned flesh were beginning to regenerate themselves. The limbs fused together into a mass of meat and bone. Collected into one giant lump, I couldn't even get it out of the furnace without having to cut them up again.

Not knowing where else to put the collection of growing limbs, I tossed it into a freezer in my art studio. There was a kitchenette down there for the times when I worked late on my sculptures and didn't want to go upstairs to cook dinner. But I never used the freezer. It was the only place I could think of to put it. I tossed the squirming ball of hands and feet into the freezer, turned the temperature to its coldest setting, and bolted the door closed.

After all that work, I still hadn't made any progress getting rid of Gabriel. He still lay there with my knife in his chest. Whole and intact. I couldn't dispose of the immortal piece by piece. I had to come up with a way to get rid of him all at once.

So I decided that trapping him would be more effective than destroying him. I mummified him in duct tape. Starting with his feet, I wrapped him in five layers of tape. Then his legs and torso and face. I removed my knife from his heart and replaced it with a scrap of metal leftover from one of my sculpture projects, then wrapped tape over the wound to forever hold it in place.

I drove his body out of town to the woods and dug a hole six feet deep. Shoveling ditches was not the kind of work I was accustomed to, but I have built up enough upper body strength from manipulating metal sculptures for so many years that I was able to accomplish the task by myself. When it was finished, I dropped the body into the hole and buried it. I thought of burning the body first, but I didn't want the smoke to attract attention. I also didn't know how effective it would be at getting rid of Gabriel. If even a small portion of his body survived the fire, he could regenerate from that. I thought it would be better to trap Gabriel—cocoon him in duct tape with a piece of metal in his heart, preventing him from reviving, then bury his body so deep he'd never escape.

It was a perfect plan. The only flaw I could see was that if anyone ever dug him up and unwrapped his bondage, he would come back to life. It would happen eventually, I was sure of that. I just hoped it didn't happen until long after my lifespan.

"So you finally got rid of him?" Edward asks Oksana.

"Had I been more careful, I would have. If the first thing I did to him was mummify his body in duct tape and bury him six feet deep, it all would have been over. The body I buried is still where I left it to this day. He would have been gone, perhaps forever. But I cut him into dozens of pieces. Any piece unaccounted for was a potential Gabriel waiting to be regenerated."

"So multiple Gabriels could be regenerated from any of the parts?"

"It was hard to believe, but yes. My attempt to get rid of him only made the situation a hundred times worse."

The moment I returned home from burying his body, I knew I'd made a horrible mistake. The smell of burning human flesh attacked my senses. Smoke filled the apartment. I was surprised the fire alarm hadn't gone off.

When I got to the kitchen, I saw the oven was propped open by a lump of meat. Foul-smelling smoke poured out and a squealing, crackling sound issued from within. I'd left it on while I was out burying the body and probably shouldn't have let it go for so long. When I looked inside, there appeared to be a ninety pound turkey baking inside the 600 degree oven. It was a mound of meat that had generated from Gabriel's severed leg. The lower section of the slab of flesh was black and charred, while the freshly grown meat was still plump and juicy, cooked to a golden brown. His limbs and head seemed to have merged with the meat, or were perhaps the blackened unrecognizable chunks on the floor of the oven. The only recognizably human features were his spine which ran across the top of the roast and his fat little rump that bubbled with juices.

I shoved the oven closed and lowered the temperature. Then I turned on the exhaust fan to get rid of the smoke. If it were just the Gabriel in the oven it would've been manageable. But there were clones growing all over the kitchen.

The toaster overflowed with oatmeal-textured flesh. It was like half-cooked pancake batter that dripped over the sides, across the counter, and down to the floor. This version of Gabriel seemed to regenerate all of his body's skin before it grew its bones and organs.

In the sink, a mass of meat and bone grew out of the drain like grotesque flowers. The fingers I had shredded in the garbage disposal created at least thirty new Gabriel clones, all of them twisting together into one entity.

A toe, which I must have dropped and lost beneath the refrigerator, was growing a tiny Gabriel fetus. The baby version of him wiggled its way out across the floor, pulsing and breathing, staring at me with its little underdeveloped eyes.

Stepping back to take in the whole scene, it was quite a horrifying sight. Dozens of mutant Gabriel blobs oozed outward, as though reaching for me. I wondered what would happen if I just let them grow. Would they eventually reform into Gabriels or would they stay grotesque and malformed? Would the Gabriels in the sink remain fused together as a mass of conjoined twins?

I wasn't sure. But I wasn't going to wait around to find out.

Getting rid of all of this flesh was not easy. If I didn't want even more of those Gabriel clones regenerating in my kitchen, cutting the meat out was the wrong approach. I had to remove the mass of flesh without creating new pieces.

"Okay, you little freak." I stood over the sink, pulling rubber gloves over my hands. "Time to get you out of there."

Three eyeballs looked up at me from the monster in the sink. There was no emotion in the eyes. They were cold. Fish eyes. The brain attached to them, hiding within a freshly developed armpit, was not fully formed yet. It did not yet possess human intelligence.

I reached into the collection of fused-together limbs, curling my fingers around a thin ankle and a meatless ribcage. Even through the gloves, I could feel the smooth fetal texture of the warm greasy flesh. It pulsed in my fingers, growing with each breath it took. I felt the blood pumping through its veins. When the clones joined together, it was like they shared the same circulatory system. One heart pumping blood through the entire mass.

Then I pulled. It wouldn't budge.

"Come on… do you really want to stay in my sink forever?"

I pulled again, trying to use my foot as leverage. The limbs unraveled as I pulled, but I couldn't get the roots of the mass free of the garbage disposal. I lifted up its side and peered into the drain to find several tiny fetus hands holding itself in place like suction cups. There were dozens of these fetal hands. They emerged from the blob, reached out to me, caressed my wrist and gripped my gloved fingers.

I jerked away from the mass of flesh, dropping it back into the sink.

Then I went down to my torture room to retrieve a couple of meat hooks. While down there, I came across more regenerating clones. Small Gabriel fetuses spilled out of the furnace, covered in ash. There was another growing out of the paint bucket, trying to crawl over the rim. Their growth wasn't as progressed as the ones upstairs. They must have generated from very small pieces. Maybe even from the chips of bone that weren't easy to burn. I decided not to worry about these clones just yet. The ones in the kitchen were a higher priority.

"Okay, Gabriels," I said upstairs, holding out my meat hooks, one in each gloved hand. "Time to be evacuated."

The mass of clones in the sink had grown almost twice as large since I'd come home. Several faces now formed on the blob of meat. Two arms were almost fully developed. The flesh was slimy, dripping with embryonic fluid. The most developed of the faces looked at me with deep eyes. It opened its mouth and gurgled at me, trying to communicate even though its vocal cords were not yet formed.

I dug the point of the meat hook deep into the garbage disposal and pulled. The tiny limbs couldn't hold on tight enough. When there was enough space freed, I gripped the bottom of the mass with the other meat hook. Then I yanked the conjoined creature out of the sink and it slapped against the kitchen floor like a fat wet fish.

I looked down at the pulsing creature on the floor. Its mostly-formed face stared back at me. Its mouth opened.

"Oksana…" His voice gurgled as fluids leaked from his lips.

I buried a meat hook deep into his skull and left it there. The last thing I needed was these things talking to me.

"Okay, freaks. What would be the best way to get rid of you?"

I really didn't know how I should get rid of them. I didn't have the time or energy to take them out to the woods and bury them. I couldn't burn them in the furnace. The only thing that sprang to mind was to drop the half-formed mutants off at the police station. The cops would freak out so much they'd bring in the military or the secret service to deal with him. The government would have the resources to destroy or at least contain Gabriel. It seemed like a decent idea, but I couldn't bring myself to do it. Too risky. Too likely to bring attention to me.

Whatever I did, I had to move fast. There was not much time before the collection of Gabriels grew to full size. It wouldn't be easy to dispose of thirty full grown men fused together into one ball of flesh. In my basement storage, I had a lot of plaster and cement that I used for art projects. About two tons of it. Burying these things in cement was probably my best option. If only I had a hole large enough to drop them into.

I should've used the dumpster in the garage, or one of the trailers I used for transporting my sculptures. Instead, I used the crawlspace under the floor of my apartment. There was a secret compartment beneath my bed, the length of a coffin but twice as deep. It was where I kept evidence of my murders. Souvenirs from my victims, newspaper clippings, an assortment of knives; it was also large enough to hold a couple prisoners if I ever felt like keeping them under me, letting their cries guide me into sleep.

Without thinking things through, I gathered up all of the regenerating clones of Gabriel and tossed them into the crawlspace. Then I filled it with cement, all the way to the top. I closed and locked the compartment, set the carpet down and rolled my bed back over it. When I was done, I collapsed on the couch and smoked probably twelve cigarettes. It finally felt as though I was rid of him. It finally felt like it was over.

Edward smiles at Oksana. He still doesn't believe a word she's saying, but he's enjoying the story anyway. He begins to realize that she's not only a brilliant artist and model, she's also a pretty good storyteller. Then again, it shouldn't be too surprising. Oksana is masterful at the art of lying. Good liars usually make good storytellers.

"But it wasn't over was it?" Edward asks her.

She taps her cigarette against the rim of her wine glass.

"No, not at all."

"You forgot a piece, didn't you?"

"I forgot a bunch of pieces."

At first, I thought it was just a normal stomach ache. I'd smoked so many cigarettes the nicotine could have made me sick. I was nauseous. I drank a glass of water. The sensation wouldn't go away. It only grew worse. My stomach twisted and turned. I could hear it gurgling loudly. I'd had food poisoning before, but this was worse. It was different. I wondered what I could have eaten that would cause such discomfort.

Then it hit me. I couldn't fucking believe it. There was no way...

Something was moving inside of my stomach.

I ran to the bathroom and lifted my shirt. I could see them through the skin. Several lumps shifted and curled inside of me. It was as though I was pregnant with a dozen babies, all kicking and rolling over at the same time. When a tiny human hand pushed against my belly, I screamed. I didn't know what else to do. I just screamed and watched my stomach rise and fall.

I'd forgotten all about the flesh I'd eaten. When there was no other way of disposing of that last piece of meat, I'd devoured it. And every single bite I took was now generating into another clone of Gabriel. He was inside of me. That son of bitch was in me and trying to tear his way out.

I didn't know how to get rid of him. I sat there for a moment, clutching my stomach, trying to hold him steady. The optimistic side of me hoped my stomach acids would be enough to stop him. I tried to trick myself into believing that I could just digest him and it would all be okay. But the realist in me knew he was regenerating faster than I could digest. He would eventually grow large enough to burst through my abdomen.

"The hospital…"

The only way to get him out would be to have him surgically removed. But could I get to the hospital in time? Was it worth the risk of exposing my secrets to the police? I'm a celebrity. There's no way that wouldn't have been all over the news. There's no way that it wouldn't generate a million questions.

A sharp pain pierced my intestines. The feeling of the worst case of diarrhea I'd ever had crawled through my system. I ran to the toilet, pulled up my skirt and ripped off my underwear. But when I raised the toilet seat, I saw Gabriel's face staring back at me. One of the body parts I'd flushed, the one that got clogged, had regenerated into another version of him. His face was warped and bent, most of it inside of the toilet bowl. The rest of his body extended through the pipes. His eyes stared up from under the water, begging me to put him out of his misery. Only his chin and mouth poked above the water, just barely, in order to breathe. Gurgling, bubbling sounds oozed from his lips. With his lungs crushed inside the pipeline, his efforts were mostly futile.

I didn't have time to get to the other bathroom, so I sat down on the toilet seat and let it out right onto his deformed face. I heard him choking and spitting as my feces covered him. But it wasn't just diarrhea coming out of me. Some of it was blood. Some of it mucus and embryonic fluid. Some of it was Gabriel.

There was a high-pitched cry as one of the Gabriel clones emerged from my asshole. It screeched and squirmed, pushing against my butt cheeks with tiny mutant hands, trying to worm its way out. I screamed as I pushed. With all my might, I tried to squeeze that living piece of shit out of me. But it wouldn't come out. I stood up off of the toilet, grabbed the human feces with my bare hand and pulled it out of me. It was lubricated with mucus, so I was able to slip him out without too much resistance. He was so long that I had to use both hands, pulling out the rope of meat one inch at a time. The sensation of sliding him out of my intestines tickled in the most unpleasant way you could imagine.

When he finally squirted out and splat against the ground, flopping violently against the tile floor, I looked down at the thing. He didn't look human at all anymore. His face was long and narrow. His limbs thin and rubbery. His eyes tightly sealed. He did not seem human. He was more like a tapeworm with arms and legs. Like some kind of alien parasite.

Another stabbing sensation in my abdomen. This wasn't the only one. There were still several more clones of Gabriel inside of me. I sat down on the toilet, pushing as hard as I could. But I couldn't shit any more of them out. They had to be removed another way.

As I went into my living room, the pressure on my stomach was getting too great. I felt heavier. They were growing inside of me, quicker by the minute. It wasn't long before they burst out of my belly.

I had no other choice. I grabbed my knife from the coffee table, sat on the couch and cut my stomach open. The human parasites exploded out of me, squirming like snakes across my chest and down my legs. Two at a time they crawled out of the wound, gasping for air.

Then I lost all my strength and dropped the knife to the couch. I'm not sure if it was from the shock or if my blade still had some residual koka juice, but I blacked out. As I slipped out of consciousness, I watched the human tapeworms wriggling against my body, latching themselves to my nipples, shrieking at me with high-pitched voices.

Oksana lifts her shirt and shows Edward where the human parasites exited her body.

"This is where I cut them out," she says.

She points at a long scar within the dragon tattoo on her abdomen.

"Is that why you got the tattoo?" Edward asks.

"I had to cover up the scar, didn't I? Even though I was no longer a model, I still couldn't live with such a hideous disfigurement. It did not heal very well. It's not easy to cut yourself open and sew yourself up."

"You didn't go to a hospital after that?"

She lowers her shirt and sits back. "A few days later I saw a cosmetic surgeon friend who fixed me up. He was the only one I trusted not to inform the media about what had happened to me. If the news learned I had been so severely wounded, there would've been too much attention on me. It was a very bad time for that to happen."

"You're lucky you survived."

Oksana laughs at his concern.

"I guess so," she says.

When I woke up, my belly was splayed wide open. Blood was everywhere. But I was still alive. Before I sewed myself up, I searched for the Gabriel parasites that had come out of me. Holding a couch cushion to my belly to stop the blood, I scanned my living room for signs of the creatures. The one in the bathroom was now the size of an alligator, but it was still long and thin like it was when it came out of me.

It squealed and moaned, making strange alien noises. The thing didn't seem to have human intelligence, perhaps because its head was so narrow. Its brain wasn't formed correctly. I found eight more of the parasites crawling through my apartment. Two of them hiding under my couch. Two in the kitchen. A few by the front door, trying to get out. I wasn't sure if I'd found them all, but I didn't have time to worry about stragglers.

I didn't have the strength to properly dispose of these clones while wounded. Instead of trying to burn them or bury them, I broke their necks one at a time and then carried them down to the basement. I threw them into the dumpster that I used for leftover scrap metal. Then I chained it shut and locked them in. They wouldn't have been able to escape and nobody would have ever heard them down there, so I figured it was the best decision under the circumstances.

Then I went upstairs and sewed myself shut.

CHAPTER NINE
NEVER LET GO

Gabriel haunted me for days after that.

I couldn't remove the version of him trapped within my plumbing, so I had to just leave him there. I taped the toilet seat shut, kept the bathroom door closed, and stuffed towels beneath the crack. But no matter what I did, I could still hear the bubbling, the gurgling. They echoed through my apartment at all hours. Even music wouldn't cover up their nerve-wracking sounds.

When I slept, I could hear the plaster cracking beneath my bed. The Gabriel clones broke through the cement as they grew, tearing my crawlspace apart. The floor of my bedroom became lumpy and misshapen. Once the cracks were wide enough for the Gabriel clones to breathe, I could hear them moaning and calling my name in warped inhuman tones. Sleeping in my bedroom became impossible, so I slept on the couch. But that still wasn't enough to escape his cries. His voices were everywhere.

Not only was it impossible to sleep, but I couldn't work anymore. The ceiling of my art studio, which was located directly beneath my bedroom, splintered into wide spiderweb fractures. Gabriel's twisted root-like limbs grew down from the ceiling. Whenever I tried to do my artwork they were always above me, reaching out for me, begging to be sliced and stabbed by the steel blades I constructed beneath him. It became so bad that I could no longer step foot in there. I couldn't work on my art, despite the deadlines I had for my next opening.

In the garage, the dumpster filled with the tapeworm-like Gabriels thrashed back and forth. The mutant clones whined and growled, slamming and scratching at the sides of the metal container, trying to break themselves out. These clones were able to grow to their full size, but they never returned to their human shape. They were monsters. Something went wrong with their regeneration process, so they stayed in their elongated tapeworm form. I didn't dare let them out. I didn't want to discover what exactly they'd grown into.

I didn't know what to do. My sanctuary was destroyed. My apartment no longer felt like home. It had become tainted with Gabriel's presence. Part of me wanted to go to a hotel so I wouldn't have to deal with him. Part of me wanted to just burn the whole place down. Or take my money and flee the country. But then Gabriel would have won. I couldn't allow that freak to beat me.

So I did the only thing I could think of doing. I grew to accept Gabriel's presence in my home. Instead of thinking of it as a curse, I treated it as a blessing. Gabriel became my muse. I took inspiration from his moans echoing through my halls. His pain and suffering motivated me. It influenced my art. Over the next couple of weeks, I created some of my best sculptures. His clones trapped in my walls became music to my ears.

It was all going fine until one night when I had too many glasses of wine. The sculptures for my next opening were finally completed and I was celebrating. Completely drunk and half-asleep on my couch, listening to opera on the radio, I didn't fully comprehend what was happening. I thought it was all just a dream. A terrible, annoying dream.

Gabriel arrived at my apartment. He unlocked the front door and casually walked inside, wearing a new suit and olive green scarf. As he strolled into the living room, he walked a dog on a leash. At least, I thought it was a dog at first. A very large, couch-sized dog.

"Hello, Oksana," Gabriel said. "I missed you."

He was his calm, angelic self again. He didn't seem angry or vengeful. He just stared at me with his deep, dark eyes.

My voice was slurred as I asked, "What the hell's that thing?"

I pointed at the dog-like creature he had on a leash. It was several mutant clones of Gabriel, mashed together into a multi-faced animal. It had six legs and an arm for a tail. It was naked except for patches of hair on random parts of its body. The creature drooled and panted at me. With its faces and brains twisted together into one, it didn't appear to have human intelligence.

"I call him Hound," Gabriel said. "He is a variation of me, an extension of my soul. He grew from the parts of me that you flushed down the toilet. They regenerated into one being down in the sewer. They were the lucky ones. Most of my clones are still trapped within the pipes. I can sense them dying and reviving again, suffering in tremendous agony."

"And where did you come from?" I asked him. "Why are you perfectly fine?"

"After he made his way out of the sewer, Hound bit off his tongue. I was able to regenerate from the tongue into my proper form. I am now the prime Gabriel."

"The prime Gabriel?"

"I can duplicate myself a million times if I wanted to, but I prefer not to. I prefer to be unique. Every once in a while I'll get into a car accident or fall from a high place, losing parts of my body that then become other Gabriels. When this happens, one of me becomes the prime. He is the one who lives in my apartment, works my job, lives the life of Gabriel. All others work as backup for the prime. They serve the prime. They do tasks the prime doesn't want to do. Basically, they become my dogs."

Hound licked Gabriel's palm with three tongues.

"Do you all share the same mind?"

"Not exactly. Whenever I'm split, the new version of me possesses all the memory and knowledge that I did at the time of the split. After that I become two completely different Gabriels and can develop completely different personalities. We can sense each other, empathize with each other, in the way some human identical twins are able to do. But we don't share the same mind anymore."

"You really aren't an angel, are you?"

I looked deep into Gabriel's eyes. He didn't have to answer me. I already knew. There was no way he was an angel. He was something else. A mutation. An alien from another planet. Maybe a rare species of man that has always existed but we only knew in myth. Perhaps he, or some immortal like him, was the origin of the vampire legend. Perhaps he was Legion, the demonic being from the bible. No matter what he really was, or where he came from, he was not a heavenly creature.

"It doesn't matter what I am," Gabriel said. "You still need me. We still had a deal."

"I made a deal with an angel, not... whatever you are. You lied to me. You're in no place to promise me entry into Heaven, if there even is such a place. The deal is null and void."

Gabriel sighed at me. Then he pulled an envelope out of his inside coat pocket.

"Very well, we'll create a new deal." He handed me the envelope.

When I opened it, I found copies of photographs. All of them were of myself murdering men. These were all from a long time ago, long before I met Gabriel. Some of them from years earlier. He had been stalking me, photographing me for a long time before we met. He was a lot scarier than I ever realized.

He said, "From now on, you will kill me and only me. If you don't then I will go to the police with these photos. You will be exposed as the Night Viper and will go to jail for the rest of your life. This is non-negotiable."

I couldn't say anything. I couldn't believe how much

documentation he had.

Gabriel pet Hound on his sweaty, lumpy back and turned away from me. "This is all I wanted to say. Next time we meet, you better be prepared to murder me. And you better make it special."

As he led Hound out of my apartment, I threw the photos at him and yelled, "Go fuck yourself, you sick freak!" I followed him out the front door. "Do you think you can blackmail me? Do you think you can *make* me kill you?" He turned back and looked at me for only a second as he waited for the elevator door to open. When it arrived, he stepped inside. I was able to get in one more sentence before the doors closed. "I don't care if I go to jail, I will never kill you ever again!" When the elevator closed, I pressed my lips against it and shouted through the crack in the door. "I'll never kill you again!"

Then I went back to my apartment and burned all the photos in my furnace.

The next day, I was so hungover I could hardly walk. My memory was foggy at that point. I kind of remember Gabriel's visit, but I brushed it off as a dream. There was no way he'd come back. He was gone for good. It was just my subconsciousness messing with me.

But I saw him again at my next art opening. Not during the opening, though I'm sure he was there somewhere, watching me. It wasn't until after the opening. I picked up a young boy who wouldn't stop talking to me about my latest series. He wasn't my typical target. He wasn't shy and meek. He was talkative, very talkative. But he had a boyish excitement to him. Perhaps it was because I hadn't killed in so long, but I wanted him badly. I *ached* to cut him open.

"You're a master, I swear," the boy said to me, wrapping his finger around the curls in his hair. "Of all the artists alive today, you're the greatest. You're the one who's going to be remembered. You're a modern day Salvador Dali. No, you're Van Gogh. But a girl. And you're so beautiful. You're the greatest, most beautiful artist ever."

I smiled and giggled, then wrapped my arm around his shoulder. "I'm glad you noticed." He was such an awkward, annoying young man. Although I was drawn to him, I wondered if it was just my desperation that made me want to kill him.

That's probably why I didn't waste much time with him. I took him into the alleyway where my car was parked. Then I reached down to squeeze his ass. But he wouldn't stop talking.

"I can't believe you want to see my portfolio. I'll show it to you next week, I swear. I'm sure you'll love it. I'm not as good as you but I'm surely just as unique."

I pulled my blade out and brushed it up his back as he spoke to me.

"You'll see. I swear you'll love my work. I had a bar display my artwork a few months ago. They took it down, but I would've showed you if it was still up. It's too bad because—"

Just as I was about to stab him in the back, his face exploded. A .45 caliber slug hit him in the side of the head, covering me in blood and bits of brain. His body fell to the street.

"What the fuck…"

I looked over to see Gabriel walking down the alley toward me. A revolver in his hand.

"I told you that you can kill only me," he said.

I looked down at the dead boy, then back at Gabriel.

"So you killed him?"

"It's better I kill him than you kill him."

I stared at the young man, imagining what it would have been like to stab him to death. I was so looking forward to cutting him open and pulling out his insides. Part of me was hoping I'd have enough time to even cut his eyeballs out and suck on them like hard candy.

"What a waste…" I said to the dead boy.

When Gabriel arrived to me, he didn't lower his weapon. He kept it pointed at me.

"It doesn't have to be a waste," he said. "You can still kill me."

I shook my head at him. "You can kill yourself, Gabriel."

I turned to walk toward my car, but was cut off by Hound. The grotesque creature stepped out of the shadows and moaned at me, drooling through its wide-open mouths. He blocked my path.

Gabriel came up behind me.

"You *will* kill me," he said.

I looked at him. He aimed his weapon at my face.

"What are you going to do, shoot me?"

"I will if you force me to."

I rolled my eyes and said, "Fine."

I stabbed him in the stomach. He fell to the ground, bleeding into the street. But he didn't die.

"You call that killing me?" His tone became angry. "You can do better than that."

"Whatever…" I said.

I cut his throat and walked away. As he bled out, an older man came into the alleyway, shocked at the sight of the two dead bodies on the street.

"What the hell's going on?" he asked. "Did you just kill that man?"

I walked past Hound and opened the door to my car.

"He's not really dead, idiot," I told him. Then I got in my car and drove away.

In the rearview mirror, I saw the old man pull out his cell phone as he went toward the dead bodies. He didn't notice Hound until it was too late. The creature lunged at him, knocked him to the ground and took the phone from him with a slobbery malformed mouth.

I looked at the foul Gabriel blood on my blade and tossed it aside. "Gross…"

Before I drove out of the alley, I looked back to see Hound on top of the screaming old man, choking and beating on him with three sets of lumpy arms. I didn't see how it all panned out, but I was pretty sure the old guy didn't last much longer.

The same thing happened three more times. I would be seconds away from killing a victim when Gabriel would interrupt and kill the boy before I could do it myself. Then he'd want me to kill him.

"I'm not killing you. Shoot me if you have to, but you can go fuck yourself."

That's what I kept saying to him. But he never shot me. He always let me walk away.

It had been so long since I'd killed anyone that I was getting desperate. I even thought about giving in and letting Gabriel be my sole murder victim again. But that wasn't going to happen. I'd rather give up killing than have to kill him.

I realized I just had to become more clever. I had to be sneakier. I decided I would find a victim in another city. I'd go on a business trip to San Francisco. Gabriel didn't have much money. He probably wouldn't be able to afford to fly across country last minute. I could. I left in the middle of the night, got on a plane and flew out within the hour. There was only one first class seat available and not another flight until the next morning. Even if Gabriel knew I was leaving, he wouldn't be able to get to me in time.

But I was wrong. When my plane landed, Gabriel was waiting for me at the gate. I was furious.

I charged up to him and said, "How the hell did you get here in time?"

"I'm just making sure you don't get the urge to kill anyone on your little trip," he said in his annoyingly calm tone.

I shouted at him in the middle of the airport. It was the middle of the night, so the terminal was mostly dead. But those who were exiting the plane behind me watched our argument.

"I'm seriously curious," I said. "How the hell did you get all the way here in time? It's not possible. There weren't any other flights."

Gabriel shook his head and put his hand on my shoulder.

"I was already here, Oksana. Gabriel called me three hours ago and told me to expect you. I've been waiting for you to arrive."

I yelled, "What do you mean Gabriel called you?"

The security guards came to me and interrupted, asked if the man was bothering me. I told them he was.

As the security escorted both of us out, Gabriel said, "I'm not the prime Gabriel. He thought you might try something like this, so he put copies of himself in every major city. There are many of us now. No matter where you go, we'll be there to stop you from breaking the deal."

The security guards listening in on the conversation had no idea what we were talking about. They probably thought we were insane.

"Are you fucking kidding me?"

I reached out to strangle the clone of Gabriel, but a security guard held me back. They took us in different directions to separate us.

"Is he an ex-boyfriend or something?" the security guard asked me.

I shook my head. "I've never met him before in my life."

But that only made the guard think I was even weirder.

I saw more and more Gabriels after that. Outside my apartment, there were always at least twelve of them staring up at me from the street. It was eerie at night, when the neighborhood was deserted. From night until morning, the street was nothing but Gabriel clones staring up at my apartment.

"Get the fuck out of here, you freaks," I yelled at them from my window. "Do you think you're going to intimidate me? Do you think you scare me?"

When I left the apartment, many of them followed me. Others stayed behind. I saw them in every restaurant I ate at. On every street corner I drove past. Whenever my art was displayed at galleries, it seemed to be mostly filled with clones of Gabriel. I have no idea how they all survived. I'm not sure where they all lived, if they had jobs, or if they were all homeless. They certainly didn't all live in Gabriel's small apartment.

One day, while I was out, they broke into my apartment and freed all the clones I had trapped in there. They dug them out of the crawlspace, freed the tapeworm-like creatures from the dumpster, and even somehow pulled out the one lodged in the toilet pipes. They kind of did me a favor, but at the same time it angered me. The idea of having some of them trapped in my apartment, suffering in horrible agony, made me feel strong. They took that away from me. It also didn't sit well with me that so many Gabriels had been in my apartment while I was gone.

I didn't feel safe anymore. They had total control of my life. There was now an army of Gabriels. It was like they'd taken over the town. I stopped seeing real people and only saw Gabriel. Even the stray dogs that usually lived in the alleyways behind my apartment had been replaced by the tapeworm-like creatures I'd locked inxp the dumpster.

I was living in a nightmare that wouldn't end.

CHAPTER TEN
END OF STORY

"How am I supposed to believe any of this?" Edward asks. "I've lived in this city all my life. If this really happened I'm sure I would have heard of stories about identical-looking men appearing all over the city. Somebody would have seen one of these mutant dog creatures lurking in the alleys."

Oksana smirks at the reporter. "You don't have to believe me if you don't want to."

"Your story is just getting ridiculous. You're just trying to fuck with me now."

"Is it working?"

Edward shakes his head.

"I don't have to continue if you don't want to hear the rest. But for your sake, you might want to."

Edward is taken aback. "What do you mean *for my sake?*"

"Don't you remember? Gabriel kills all the men I target as victims. You are one of my targets. How do you know he's not going to come after you?"

"Because he's not real."

"Are you sure?" She lifts her shirt and points to her belly. "Do think I scarred myself for nothing?"

Gabriel shakes his head. "That could have been from anything. One of your victims could have fought back."

"Suit yourself," she says. "If you're not interested in my story we can talk about something else. Want to know about my days of modeling in Paris? I have a great story about an evening I spent with Karl Lagerfeld."

"No, I don't think so."

Oksana rubs her hands down her legs and gives him a seductive, hungry stare. "Well, we can always play if you're through with the interview. I'm getting tired of talking anyway. I want to feel your blood on my lips…"

Edward's hand trembles as he aims his gun at the model. "Don't even think about it."

She continues touching herself, rubbing her legs and tattooed stomach. Then she takes her knife from the table and holds it in her lap as though it were an erection.

"You look so pathetic with a gun in your hand," she tells him, rubbing a finger up the edge of her blade. "You should really just put it down and give in. You're going to have to eventually anyway. We both know you're never going to get out of here alive."

Edward tries to change the subject. It's safer for him to keep her focused on telling the story.

"So Gabriel's still out there?" he asks. "Does he still try to kill your prey?"

"So you believe me now? Are you worried he's going to get you before I can?"

"I might as well hear the whole story."

"Well, you should know that answer already. The newspapers have reported dozens of Night Viper murders since then. I've obviously gotten back to killing without his interruptions."

"Did you ever end up killing anyone while Gabriel was around?"

Oksana sits back. She gives up on seducing Edward, but doesn't let go of her knife. "I wasn't able to enjoy murdering until after he was out of the picture."

"So he was always able to stop you?"

Oksana nods her head but then stops part of the way through. "Although, there was this one time…"

I was resolved to give up on murder for a while. For over a month, I didn't attempt to kill anyone. I ignored Gabriel's clones. I mostly stayed home and worked on my sculptures. That was when I started the human mousetrap series. It was partially inspired as a way to kill men without Gabriel interfering. If my sculptures killed my victims then Gabriel couldn't do anything about it.

My goal was pretty much to just move on with my life and hope that someday Gabriel would lose interest in me. It seemed to be working. I saw fewer and fewer of his clones hanging out around my apartment. Fewer and fewer followed me around town. Even if it took years, I figured he would eventually give up. Perhaps that was what he was thinking as well. Perhaps he was just waiting for my urge to kill to come back and hoping that I would come to him to rekindle our relationship.

My life had become more peaceful. More relaxing and productive. I mostly just stayed home, ordering takeout from the Indian food restaurant down the street. Gabriel never attempted to enter my apartment again. I had a new security system installed and all the locks changed. He either couldn't get in or didn't try.

One night, I ordered some goat curry and vegetable samosas for dinner. The delivery boy was this cute Indian guy. Short and thin with curly black hair. He had facial hair, but it was clean and well-trimmed. That night I was busy creating blueprints for a new sculpture I was about to get started on. I sat in my robe with my reading glasses on. My hair was a mess. When he arrived at my place, I rang him up. I didn't want to pause what I was doing for a second, so I let him bring the food to me.

"You're late," I told him as he entered my apartment.

He just nodded at me and brought me my food. I looked down at it, then up at him. He had a calm, innocent expression on his face.

"Why don't you serve it to me?" I told him. "There are plates in the kitchen."

He nodded and did as I asked. I couldn't believe he was actually serving me in my own home. He probably thought he'd get a big tip. It was so cute. I couldn't get the smile off of my face as I raised my reading glasses up the bridge of my nose.

As he looked for dishes in my kitchen, I removed my glasses and admired his ass. I set down my blueprints. No longer interested in work. That's when I realized what I had in my possession. A cute young boy was in my apartment and there was no Gabriel in sight. I could do whatever I wanted to him.

Of course, there was a problem. Killing him would point the cops in my direction, because they would know he was scheduled for a delivery to my apartment when he disappeared. But I was so turned on, so desperate to taste his blood, that I didn't care about the consequences. I'd figure all that out later.

"They're in the third cabinet on the top left," I called to him. "Get an extra plate for yourself."

He looked at me with a confused expression.

"You're hungry, aren't you? Stay with me a while. I could use the company."

"I'll get in trouble," he said.

He had a strange accent. It was more European than Indian.

"Don't worry about that. I'll talk to your boss about it. The amount I pay will more than make up for your lost time."

He brought the food on two plates and placed them on the living room coffee table. As he went to the seat across from me, the seat you're sitting in now, I shook my head and told him not to sit there. I moved over and told him to sit next to me.

My robe was open when he sat down, my black lace underwear visible between my slightly parted thighs. He averted his eyes, too nervous to look, focusing instead on the food.

"You look too hot in that jacket," I told him. "Take it off."

I didn't wait for him to do as I ask and took it off for him. Then pressed myself close to his body and looked him in the eyes. I leaned in as though to kiss him. Then I said, my breath on his face, "You look far more delicious than the food you brought me."

He opened his mouth to kiss me, but I pulled back.

"Can you get something for me really quickly?" I asked. "It's on the shelf over there."

He nodded and quickly did as I said. The boy thought he was going to get laid. He would've done anything for me.

"What do you want?" he asked, scanning the bookcase.

As he searched the shelf, I placed a sheet of plastic down on the floor. "It's the one with the handle that looks like a tentacle."

He saw my knife sitting on the shelf and lifted it up. "This?"

I nodded at him. "That's the one. Bring it here."

"What is it?" he asked, as he brought the knife to me and handed it over.

I didn't answer his question.

"Sit down," I told him, pointing at the plastic-covered floor. "I don't want to make a mess."

He did as I asked. He was absolutely clueless. It was the most fun I'd had in a long time.

When he kneeled down, my crotch was at his eye-level. I stepped forward until my panties were inches from his face, then I just stared down at him for a moment, admiring him kneeling before me. I'm not sure if it was the scent of me or if I sent the wrong signals, but he suddenly lost his shyness and took initiative. He slipped off my underwear and grabbed my ass, pulling me toward his face.

I'd never killed anyone while receiving oral sex before. It wasn't something I was normally into. I never had sex with my victims. That just wasn't anything that ever appealed to me before. But he was so accommodating, so thirsty and willing. I laid him on his back and sat on top of his face, allowing him to lick me as I caressed my blade above him. It was meant as a distraction as I formulated a method for eviscerating him, but I found myself getting into it. For me, it was foreplay. As I came closer to orgasm, the anticipation grew. I held the knife over him, ready to drop it into his skull at any second. Knowing that he would die with his tongue inside of me only turned me on more. It was such an exhilarating sensation.

I held my knife in the air, pressing my weight against him, grinding his head into the ground. But then I decided I didn't want to stab him in the head. I wanted to stab him in the chest. So I turned around to face the other direction, switching positions on his face so fast I nearly broke his neck. Then he continued licking, faster, focusing on just the right spot.

I opened up his shirt and rubbed my hand across his chest. I grabbed and clawed at his ribs, twisting at his nipples. When he jerked from the pain, it only made me come faster. Just before I reached orgasm, I thrust the knife into his chest. A geyser of blood sprayed into the air as I pulled the blade out. Then I stabbed him again and again as I came against his face. He didn't stop licking me. Even as I mutilated him, he continued pleasing me with his tongue. It was as though he didn't care about his own death and wanted to use his last fleeting seconds of life to make sure I was gratified. It made me come a second time.

When I was finished, I sighed with relief. I needed that. I really, really needed that. After months of abstention, I was finally able to satisfy my cravings. I stood up, admiring his dead body on my floor. Gabriel wasn't able to stop me. I finally killed someone worth killing.

But then I noticed something odd. The man's skin on his torso was pale, much paler than the skin on his face. I examined closer. His body didn't match his face at all. The skin clashed too much. When I saw the wounds on his body closing up and healing themselves, I couldn't believe it. I stepped back and screamed at the corpse.

"You weaselly motherfucker!" I yelled at him. "How could you do this to me?"

When he was healed and regained consciousness, he sat up and looked at me.

"Gabriel?" I pulled on my underwear and tightened my robe. "How the hell could that be you?"

He shook his head. "I'm sorry I had to deceive you." He still had the voice of the delivery boy. He really didn't look anything like Gabriel anymore. "This wasn't supposed to happen."

"You're able to change your face?"

He shook his head. "Not exactly. I'm not actually the prime Gabriel. After you ordered so much food from the Indian food place, the prime asked me to replace him. So that I could keep an eye on you. I've been delivering your food to you for the past week or so."

"How did you do it?"

"I killed your real delivery boy and cut off his face. I grafted his skin onto my own. It required removing my own face, which was much more painful and complicated than you'd think, but the delivery boy's skin easily fused with my own. I also took his voice box and made it mine, although I don't sound exactly like the original. It's been enough to fool his employers and roommates, though. I've taken over his life since then."

He cleaned the blood from his chest using paper napkins from the Indian restaurant. Then he buttoned his shirt. Once his Gabriel skin was no longer showing, he really did look like a completely different person. At first I was disgusted that the delivery boy was really Gabriel in disguise, but then I thought about it. It was still an amazing kill. I enjoyed every second of it.

"If you did this kind of thing more often then I wouldn't have broken off our deal," I told him.

"What do you mean?" he asked.

"If you took on the appearance of other men, made me think I was killing somebody new each time, then our relationship wouldn't have grown old."

"Are you serious?" he asked.

I went to him and touched his cheek. It really felt like another person's cheek. Despite being Gabriel, he didn't remind me of Gabriel at all.

"I might be willing to kill you more often if this is how you did it."

He looked at me, his mouth wide open. Then he sighed. He looked away and shook his head. "I can't."

"Why not?" His answer was a surprise.

"I'm not the prime Gabriel. *He's* the one you're supposed to kill. If he found out that you have already killed me instead of him he will be furious."

I laughed at him. It was a hilarious relationship Gabriel had with himself.

"But don't you want to be killed by me as much as he does?" I asked.

"Of course I do."

"Then why don't you just kill the prime Gabriel and take over?"

"Kill the prime?"

"Not just the prime. Kill *all* the other Gabriels. Get rid of them and it can just be the two of us. What do you say?"

He looked down and thought about it. His mind was so conflicted. The idea of becoming the only Gabriel and becoming my only murder victim was obviously what he wanted more than anything in the world.

"Okay," he said, nodding at me. "I'll do it. I'll kill the other Gabriels for you."

I smiled at him.

"Once they're all dead, we can start again. We'll figure something out that will work for us. I'm sure it will work out." He stepped forward. "Do you want to kill me when I deliver your food next time?"

I pushed him back. "No, that's not how it's going to work. I don't want to kill you unless I don't know it's actually you. You'll have to disguise yourself as other men. It has to be exactly as it was tonight."

He nodded. "Okay."

"Just kill the other Gabriels and then we'll talk."

"Okay."

He was so excited he could barely talk. He just bowed at me and walked backwards. Then he ran out of my apartment like he'd just won the lottery.

He wasn't the only Gabriel I made that deal with. Every clone I came across I convinced to do the exactly the same thing. It was how I was able to get the upper hand on that immortal freak. I turned him against himself. Gabriels were at war with other Gabriels. They killed each other and disposed of their bodies. If anyone knew how to permanently kill a Gabriel it was another Gabriel. And I didn't have to do a thing. I just sat back and waited for them to all be killed off.

Only Gabriel knew how many other Gabriels were out there, so he was able to seek and destroy every single one of them. He left not a single version of himself alive. In the meantime, I was able to start killing again. The Gabriels were so focused on waging war with each other that they didn't realize what I was doing behind their backs.

I'd never felt more triumphant in all my life.

"So that's it?" Edward asks. "That's the whole story."

Oksana nods. "Basically. That's how I finally got rid of Gabriel."

Edward stares at her for a minute. Then shakes his head. "But that didn't get rid of him. Even if you tricked all his clones into killing each other, there would still be at least one of them left. What happened to the final Gabriel?"

Oksana smiles. "I still have him."

"You still have him?"

She nods. "Would you like to see? I keep him downstairs."

Edward laughs. "I'm not stupid enough to fall for that one. Do you actually think I'll follow you downstairs into some kind of trap you have in store for me?"

"There's no trap. If you're going to expose my secret life to the world, you might as well have the full story."

Edward keeps his gun pointed at her, unable to decide whether to trust her or not. But his curiosity gets the best of him.

"Very well, but leave the knife here. And if it even kind of seems like you're going to try anything I won't hesitate to shoot you."

She nods at him. Then she stabs her knife into the table and takes a coat from the coat rack.

"Follow me."

They take the elevator down one floor and Oksana leads the reporter through a dimly lit hallway. Edward's sure she's planning something. He's sure she's going to jump him when his attention is distracted or push him into one of her human mousetrap sculptures. So he moves carefully, watching her every move.

"This way," she says. "To my workshop."

"What are you going to show me?" he asks.

"You'll see."

Edward pauses and waits for her to turn around. "The mystery is making me jumpy. At least give me a hint."

She looks at Edward, blinks languidly and smiles. "Do you remember I said that there was one piece of Gabriel that I disposed of by tossing into my workshop freezer?"

Edward nods.

"Well, it is one piece that I forgot about for the longest time.

I never use that freezer. It took me forever to find it again. When there was only one Gabriel left and he was busy trying to disguise himself with the face of another random young man, I figured out what I would do with him. The piece of Gabriel I left in the freezer regenerated in such a curious way. It grew like a collection of curled icicles, reaching out in all directions before it froze solid. I thought it was beautiful. A work of art. It was the perfect inspiration for my next series."

Edward's mouth drops open. "You couldn't possibly mean…"

"You'll be the first to see it," she says. "My next exhibition will send shockwaves through not only the art world, but through all of human society. No one will ever forget the name Oksana Maslovskiy after these pieces are revealed."

She opens the door to her workshop and steps inside. Edward follows.

"Edward, meet Gabriel," she says as the reporter enters the room. "My living art series."

When Edward sees it, he can't believe his eyes. The room is full of over a dozen massive sculptures. All of them are made of flesh and bone.

Edward steps forward, his eyes unable to blink. The sculptures gurgle and moan at him. The human forms have been twisted into abstract works of art. Intricate and surreal shapes that remind him of a Holocaust memorial, starkly beautiful and yet twisted and dark.

"How is it possible?" he asks.

Oksana can't get enough of the expression on the young man's face. "I discovered a way to dry-freeze his flesh. It doesn't kill him, but it prevents him from regenerating after I've molded him into the shape I desire."

Edward steps close to a sculpture and touches it. There are about ten Gabriel clones melded together into what almost appears to be a Chinese dragon sculpture. Twenty eyes stare angrily at the reporter as he touches the scaled flesh.

"Gabriel's immortal flesh is my favorite material I've ever

worked with to create artwork. Better than steel or clay. And I had an unlimited supply. Whenever I needed more, I would just cut a piece off of him and place him into a mold. His body would grow into the shape of the mold, then it would be freeze-dried and stitched to the rest of the sculpture."

No matter how long he looks at it, he still can't believe it.

"It's insane..."

Oksana smiles. "Isn't it? It's my greatest work. I'll be remembered forever for this."

Edward turns to her. "You're actually going to display this?"

"Of course. Why wouldn't I?"

"They're living beings. They won't let you display this. You'll be arrested."

"Maybe I will, but not right away. Nobody will actually believe these are real humans in my artwork. Not at first, at least. Who would believe it? They will swear that it has to be some kind of special effect. Either way, people will talk about it. Eventually they'll learn the truth."

"But they won't let you get away with this. The government will take them away. They'll want to study him."

"Perhaps. But by then there will be thousands of photos and videos spread all over the world. These sculptures will live and never be forgotten. They'll be even more immortal than Gabriel himself."

Edward shakes his head and backs away from the sculpture. "I'm leaving."

"You can't leave," Oksana says.

"Why not?" Edward asks.

"Because I haven't had you yet."

Oksana steps toward him. Edward steps back. He aims his gun at her head.

As his weapon trembles at her, Oksana smiles at him and rolls her eyes.

"You're such a tease," she says. Then she reaches into her robe.

Edward almost pulls the trigger, thinking she's going for a

weapon, but she holds out a car key.

"Take this," she says, and tosses the key toward him.

The gun nearly goes off as he catches it.

"You can have whichever car that belongs to. I don't need it anymore."

Edward looks down at the key, confused. "You're letting me go?"

"Disappointed? You can take a rain check if you like."

Edward shakes his head.

"The thing is I want you to get my story out. I want people to know everything about me. This next exhibit is going to be earth-shattering. And if you get my story out that's only going to make it all the more significant."

"So you want to be exposed as the Night Viper?"

"I would've been caught eventually. It might as well be at the height of my popularity."

The sculptures moan at Edward. He cringes at their sounds, tries to block them out.

"You have exclusive rights to my story, young Edward," she says. "Just give me a few months. These works won't be revealed until then. I'd rather have my timing just right."

Edward nods.

"Though you might want to watch your back in the meantime," Oksana says. "You never know, I might change my mind. It would be so much fun to put my blade inside your smooth, milky skin."

Edward takes a deep breath. He can't believe she's actually letting him go.

"The next time I see you, I won't hesitate to shoot," he says.

"I'll keep that in mind," she says.

Then a wide smile appears on Oksana's face.

Edward rushes out of there as soon as he can and doesn't look back. He takes the elevator to the basement and props it open with a cinderblock so that she can't follow after him. The basement is as dark as it was when they arrived. He hits the remote switch on the keychain but the lights don't come on. There is a miniature flashlight on the keychain that he has to use to find his way.

The garage is much more frightening than it was on the way in. Every mannequin he passes, he thinks might be Oksana standing with her knife raised at him. Every piece of garbage he crosses, he imagines is a half-regenerated piece of Gabriel crawling across the ground. When he passes the dumpsters, he swears that they're still filled with tapeworm-shaped creatures from Oksana's story. It's all in his imagination, of course, but he refuses to lower his pistol for even a second.

When he hits the unlock button on the keys, the lights of a yellow sports car brighten his path. He goes to it, gets in and starts it up. The whole time he watches the elevator and the door to the stairwell, making sure that Oksana doesn't come after him.

He pulls out of the parking spot and drives up the ramp to the garage exit. The moment the garage door opens and he turns out onto the street, he sighs with relief. He's actually out of there. He actually pulled it off.

"You did it," he says to himself. "How the fuck did you actually do it?"

He stops the car at the next light, and looks down at his phone. Everything seems to have been recorded okay. He sends all of the files to his email, just in case. This information is the most valuable thing he'll ever own.

As the light turns green, Edward looks up at a hideous face staring at him through the windshield. Not just one face, actually, but three faces melded together. He drops the phone in his lap when he sees it.

"What, the…"

Standing in the crosswalk, blocking his path, is a horrible creature made out of Gabriel clones. Edward's sure it's the one from Oksana's story. The creature called Hound. He looks exactly as she described.

Edward doesn't know what to do. He just stares at the creature, and the creature stares back, thick ropes of mucus leak from its nostrils and mouths. The thing can't get him inside the car. At least, Edward hopes it can't. He should be safe, but the last thing he feels is safety.

"This isn't happening. This isn't happening…"

A knock on the driver side window makes him scream out loud. He looks over to see a young man with a gun. Judging by his thin figure and deep dark eyes, Edward's sure he knows who the man is. Oksana must not have gotten rid of all of the Gabriel clones. There's a new prime walking the streets.

"What do you want?" Edward asks.

Gabriel looks at him with calm, ancient eyes. "Your phone. Hand it over?"

Edward decides to act stupid. "Is this a robbery?"

"I can't allow Oksana's story to get out," he says. "She doesn't know what she's doing."

"Were you spying on us?"

Gabriel points the gun at him through the glass. "Just hand it over."

Edward rolls down the window just a crack and tosses the phone out on the street. He's happy he was able to email himself copies of the files before this encounter. Otherwise, he would've been in trouble.

"Now get out of the car," Gabriel says.

Edward panics. "What?"

"Get out."

"What for?"

"I need something from you."

Edward doesn't know what to do. He remembers the story Oksana told about how Gabriel's clones would steal the faces of men she was attracted to. He wonders if that's what Gabriel has planned for him. He decides that has to be it.

"Don't shoot, I'm coming out."

Edward looks at Hound as the creature licks mucus from its lips with three tongues. Then it pants at him.

Gabriel lowers his weapon and steps back, waiting for Edward to get out. That's when the reporter makes his move. He kicks the door open with all his strength, slamming it right into Gabriel's knees. Hound growls and slobbers as Gabriel loses his balance.

Edward doesn't hesitate. Before Gabriel can shoot, Edward points his own pistol at the immortal's head and fires four times. Gabriel's face explodes with blood as he falls to the street. Edward gets back into the vehicle before Hound can react.

"Shit, shit, shit…" Edward cries to himself. He doesn't even realize he's saying it.

He slams on the gas and rams straight into Hound, then runs the creature over. The thing's so large it's like trying to run over a moose, but he manages to get over it. He speeds down the road without looking back.

"What the fuck, what the fuck, what the fuck," he says as he races as far away as he can get.

Gabriel has his phone. He'll find out where he lives. Edward decides not to go back to his apartment. He has to get out of town. He has to get as far away as he possibly can.

There's a hotel on a back highway he knows of. He can stay there for now. He has an old high school friend that's going to school in the next state that's been begging him to visit forever. Edward can stay there for a few days. Then he'll go out west. He knows plenty of people who can help him out.

Edward wipes the tears from his eyes. He thinks he'll be safe. He thinks Gabriel will never be able to find him. He thinks he'll get his story out, it will get published, and he'll forever be known for uncovering the true identity of the Night Viper serial killer. It will make his career as a journalist. It will ensure him a spot in the history books.

If only he knew about the six pieces of Hound's flesh stuck to the bottom of the vehicle, growing into six new Gabriels that would stop at nothing to erase him from the face of the planet.

BONUS SECTION

This is the part of the book where we would have published an afterword by the author but he insisted on drawing a comic strip instead for reasons we don't quite understand.

I hope you liked my new book *As She Stabbed Me Gently in the Face.*

Wasn't it just lovely?

It's me CM3!

This year I wrote more than I ever had in my life.

I wrote eight books between February and June, which means I wrote two years worth of releases in less than half a year.

I was so burned out after that experience that I couldn't do much more than play Minecraft and watch K-dramas for the rest of the summer.

My favorite K-drama is called *Everlasting Pineapple Prince*. It's about a girl who falls in love with an adorable pineapple that is actually a prince.

Sometimes the prince is in human form but even in human form he still has that spiky pineapple skin that is kind of gross and awkward and prickly when they kiss.

For most of the show, the girl loves the pineapple prince more than anyone in the whole world.

Then she gets bored and chops him up and eats him.

It's kind of a dumb show but it's really addicting to watch. In fact, once I started it I couldn't stop.

I was browsing k-dramas on Hulu one afternoon and decided to throw it on while eating a bowl of Christmas Crunch.

37 hours later I was crying my eyes out at the conclusion of the show. I hadn't slept, eaten or bathed in days.
It was just that addicting.

Some people think k-dramas are lame and cliché, but I'm kind of envious of the writers of these shows. It takes incredible skill to addict your audience like this and I think one of the most important aspects of writing is getting your audience addicted to your stories.

That's why I lace the pages of my books with concentrated heroin.

THE END

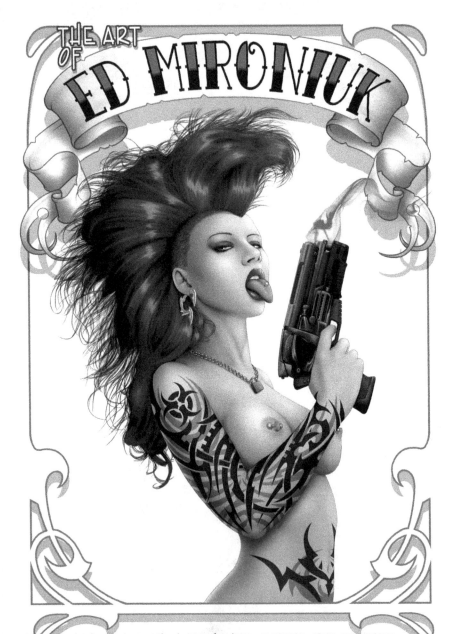

ABOUT THE AUTHOR

Carlton Mellick III is one of the leading authors of the
bizarro fiction subgenre. Since 2001, his books have drawn
an international cult following, despite the fact that they have
been shunned by most libraries and chain bookstores.

He won the Wonderland Book Award for his novel, *Warrior
Wolf Women of the Wasteland*, in 2009. His short fiction has
appeared in *Vice Magazine, The Year's Best Fantasy and
Horror #16, The Magazine of Bizarro Fiction,* and *Zombies:
Encounters with the Hungry Dead,* among others. He is also
a graduate of Clarion West, where he studied under the likes
of Chuck Palahniuk, Connie Willis, and Cory Doctorow.

He lives in Portland, OR, the bizarro fiction mecca.

Visit him online at **www.carltonmellick.com**